"A penny for your thoughts," Mr. Harrison Montgomery said quietly, close to Charlotte's ear. "What think you of the telescope?"

"Only a penny?" she asked, closing the instrument and shutting the case with a definite snap. "I gather you mean to make sport of me, sir, so I protest that a penny is rather a miserly price for your entertainment."

His gray eyes teased her lightly. "Make sport of you? Upon my oath, ma'am, nothing was further from my mind."

Placing no faith in his vow, she did not give her opinion; she changed the subject.

"Did *you* not find the view through the glass wonderful?"

He did not answer right away. Instead, he gazed at her so long and so intently that she grew nervous and longed to avert her eyes. But she had never looked away first in her life, and she would not do so now.

He finally let his gaze slip down to her mouth.

"Not fair," he whispered. "I offered you a penny for your thoughts, yet you sought mine without proposing so much as a farthing in return. Had you another form of payment in mind?"

Mr. Montgomery's Quest

Martha Kirkland

A SIGNET BOOK

SIGNET
Published by New American Library, a division of
Penguin Putnam Inc., 375 Hudson Street,
New York, New York 10014, U.S.A.
Penguin Books Ltd, 27 Wrights Lane,
London W8 5TZ, England
Penguin Books Australia Ltd, Ringwood,
Victoria, Australia
Penguin Books Canada Ltd, 10 Alcorn Avenue,
Toronto, Ontario, Canada M4V 3B2
Penguin Books (N.Z.) Ltd, 182–190 Wairau Road,
Auckland 10, New Zealand

Penguin Books Ltd, Registered Offices:
Harmondsworth, Middlesex, England

First published by Signet, an imprint of New American Library,
a division of Penguin Putnam Inc.

First Printing, October 2001
10 9 8 7 6 5 4 3 2 1

Copyright © Martha Cotter Kirkland, 2001
All rights reserved

 REGISTERED TRADEMARK—MARCA REGISTRADA

PUBLISHER'S NOTE
This is a work of fiction. Names, characters, places, and incidents either
are the product of the author's imagination or are used fictitiously,
and any resemblance to actual persons, living or dead, business
establishments, events, or locales is entirely coincidental.

*To Rosemarie Kerekgyarto, a warmhearted lady
with a generous spirit and a wonderful sense
of humor. A great Hungarian cook, she loved
classical music (especially Franz Liszt)
and Regency romances. This book is for
"Rosie" and for her daughters, who
carry her in their hearts.*

Chapter One

"Heaven be praised," Miss Charlotte Pelham murmured, "for I believe the postboy is reining in the horses at last."

The young gentleman who sat in the forward seat gave her a telling look. "If you can say 'heaven' and 'postboy' in the same breath, Charlotte, then we could not have been riding in the same chaise. On my oath, when I consider the devilish experience the yahoo just put us through, I can only conclude that this must be his first day riding post."

Charlotte was of a similar opinion, for at no time had they traveled faster than four miles per hour, yet the wheels of the hired chaise had bounced over every rut and every stone in the road. Not that she required luxury, or even the usual comforts. If ease had been her goal, she would have remained at home in Lancashire, instead of trekking across the entire country with two youths, on what her mother's new husband had referred to as the most harebrained scheme ever concocted.

"Furthermore," the young gentleman continued, "when I get my hands on that uncommonly lucky brother of yours, I mean to have a look at that coin he tossed. I believe the cursed thing has two heads."

"The coin, or my brother?"

"Both!"

Charlotte chuckled, though she, too, envied her

brother his ride on horseback. Since the "yellow
bounder" held only two passengers, she and her two
companions had tossed a coin to see who rode horseback the final few miles of their journey. Not that
the hired hack had looked all that sweet mouthed.
Still, her brother had been in the open air, while she
and their friend had been cooped up inside the
wretchedly sprung chaise, bouncing to and fro, and
obliged to pretend they did not smell the still-
lingering aroma of the previous passenger's meal of
onions and goat cheese.

The chaise, trailing the horse and rider by at least
a quarter of an hour, passed beneath the gaily col-
ored sign of the White Rose Inn and came to a lurch-
ing stop in the inn yard. Only too happy to quit the
conveyance, Charlotte's friend lost no time in flinging
open the door and bounding to the ground. Though
he was still boyishly slender and only a few inches
taller than Charlotte's five-foot-five inches, he turned
and caught her by her waist, and with the familiarity
of one who has known her for most of his fifteen
years, he lifted her out and set her on her feet.

Charlotte still had not grown accustomed to the
fact that during the boys' final year at Eton, both
Jonathan and Peter had passed her by in height as
well as strength. For as long as she could remember,
she had bested her brother and his friend at every
sport, but that had not been marvelous, for she was
nine years their senior and unconventionally athletic
for a female. Now, however, it appeared that nature
was about to even the score.

She was still marveling at the way the two youths
had grown, when the scarlet-coated postboy jumped
down from the lead horse and came forward, slap-
ping his fluffy beaver hat against his white corduroy
breeches to rid it of the dust from the road. " 'Ere

you be, miss," he said, pointing westward. "St. Bee's Head lies just yonder. 'Alf a mile down t'road."

Allowing her gaze to follow the fellow's pointing finger, Charlotte strained to see any signs of the Cumbrian seacoast. When still a young girl, she had visited the village of St. Bee's on numerous occasions, just she and her father, but the White Rose Inn was tucked behind a series of rolling hills, allowing not even a glimpse of the red sandstone cliffs or the magnificent clifftop view of Solway Firth.

She breathed deeply, imagining she could smell the fresh, salty air of the Firth and the Irish Sea. Lamenting the lack of time to travel that extra half mile, she contented herself with the knowledge that in the next fifteen days she would see enough varied scenery to satisfy even the most ardent nature lover. Early tomorrow she would begin a coast-to-coast walking tour, covering roughly 190 miles from the Irish Sea to the North Sea.

For just a moment, she closed her eyes, wondering if she was, indeed, equal to the task she had set herself. Of course, it was too late now for doubts. She *had* to be equal to the task for many reasons, not the least of which were the eight people waiting inside the rambling, gray stone inn, waiting for her, their leader.

Not that any of the eight knew they were waiting for her. It was *Charles* Pelham they were expecting, a name Charlotte had used in her correspondence with Bonaventure Tours, the London travel service, to secure the position as guide for Bonaventure's first-time-ever west to east walking tour.

Charlotte had only just opened her eyes when she heard the sound of hooves behind her. Thinking it might be one of the members of the tour, she turned, a ready smile on her face. What she saw passing beneath the inn sign was a handsome roan gelding,

pulling an equally handsome maroon-and-gold Tilbury.

Two men occupied the seat of the gig. The small,
swarthy-skinned man to the right wore a turban with
a jeweled broach pinned just above his forehead and
a long white coat over some sort of polished silk
breeches that were gathered around the ankles.
Though he was unusual enough to catch anyone's
attention, one look at the tall, broad-shouldered gentleman who handled the ribbons with such skill, and
Charlotte saw nothing else. The driver, dressed in a
beautifully cut slate blue coat, gray breeches, and a
gray curly brim beaver, was unquestionably the most
impressive man Charlotte had ever seen. Breathtakingly impressive.

She did a mental run-through of the list of names
of the gentlemen on the tour. Not one of those names
seemed to fit the man in the Tilbury.

Charlotte had spent the entire twenty-four years of
her life in the little village of Burley, in Lancashire,
some sixty miles south, and there was not a male
in the entire village she could not outrun, outswim,
outride, or outshoot. As a result, none of the gentlemen of her acquaintance had ever shown the least
interest in paying his addresses to Charlotte, or of
seeking her hand for a dance at the local assemblies.
Not that she had cared overmuch.

Now, however, as she watched the driver of the Tilbury rein in the roan, hand the ribbons to the strange-
looking man beside him, then leap to the ground,
she knew why she had never cared if the men of
Burley sought other partners at the dances. She had
been waiting for just such a man as this.

None of the men in her village could match this
stranger's height, nor his physique. He was well over
six feet, he weighed at least thirteen stone, and judging by the unmistakable movement of muscles be-

neath his finely tailored coat, she would bet her last shilling that every inch of his body was as hard as the river stones used in the construction of the White Rose Inn.

The stranger strode toward the studded oak entrance, his powerful legs making short work of the distance, and as he moved, confidence surrounded him like some mystical aura. Just looking at him made Charlotte's heartbeat quicken. Here was a man who would command respect, a man who had probably never been bested by anyone.

Here was the man of her dreams!

If the gentleman saw in her the woman of his dreams, however, he hid the fact well. Though he gave her a slow and thoroughly appraising look that measured her from head to foot, his hard-edged, enigmatic features revealed nothing. He studied her traveling companion as well, and here, too, the stranger kept his thoughts to himself. Her friend appeared unmoved by the man's appraisal, but Charlotte found her heart beating rapidly just knowing those cool gray eyes had skimmed her figure.

Just before the man reached the entrance to the inn, the door swung open and Charlotte's brother stepped out, a cheeky grin on his youthful face. "What kept you two?" he asked, feigning a yawn of boredom. "I vow I have been here an age."

The man turned his attention to the new arrival, staring at him, then looking once again toward Charlotte's friend, an expression of incredulity on his face. Charlotte was not surprised at the man's confusion, for the boys were of similar height and build, and like her, they both possessed black hair and dark brown eyes. People unacquainted with the family often mistook the boys for brothers; some even thought them twins.

The postboy chose that moment to hold out his

hand for the expected gratuity, and Charlotte was obliged to return her thoughts to the business that had brought her to St. Bee's, Cumbria. While she counted coins into the fellow's rather grimy palm, the stranger entered the inn, lost perhaps forever to the woman who had admired him from afar.

Being quite fond of her brother, Charlotte said nothing about the discomfort of her ride, but their friend, unhampered by bonds of brotherly loyalty, gave vent to his feelings. "Here, you rotter," he said, "give us a look at that coin you seem always so eager to toss."

"My coin?" her brother asked. "Whatever can you mean by—"

"Stubble it, Captain Sharp, for I have come to suspect both you and that coin. Seems to me you've been uncommonly lucky of late, and I say you empty your pockets right here and now."

It was too much to hope that two young gentlemen who had been playfellows from the age of four, and had gone off to school together, would show each other the least respect, so Charlotte was not surprised when a round of name-calling ensued. Afraid they were not above falling to the ground in a friendly tussle, she reminded them that she had brought them along as paid assistants to her in this rather uncertain venture, not to offer entertainment for the stable hands. "And remember, if you please, that you are both supposed to be my brothers—my two *youngest* brothers."

"Sorry," they said as one, and moments later, when Charlotte entered the inn, they followed close behind her, both young gentlemen ready to play the parts agreed upon.

"Good day," Charlotte said to the short, rotund landlord who stood behind a heavy wood counter. Room keys hung from a row of pegs on the wall behind the man, and a thick ledger lay open on the counter. Obviously, the tall gentleman from the Tilbury had just signed his name in the ledger, for the landlord was returning an ink-dampened pen to a small pewter tray when Charlotte spoke.

"Yes, miss? Can I do ought for ye?"

"I am Miss Pelham," she said, "and these are my brothers. We are to lead a party of cross-country walkers from St. Bee's, here on the Irish Sea, to Robin Hood's Bay, on the North Sea. I believe you corresponded with my older brother, Mr. Charles Pelham, about supplying the rooms for the Bonaventure Tours for this first night."

"I did," the landlord replied. "Is Mr. Pelham still outside?"

Charlotte had been expecting this question. She had rehearsed her reply many times before the looking glass in her bedchamber at the vicarage, but when she finally spoke the lines aloud, they sounded false even to her own ears. "Is my brother not here already?"

"No, miss, he b'aint here. Nor've I glimmed eyes on him."

"Ah, then he must have, er, been delayed. He told me that in such an event, he would, er, meet us tomorrow at the Ghyll Inn at Ambleside."

The little rotund man gave her a look that said he had been lied to by the best, and that he did not believe a word she said. "If Mr. Pelham be at the Ghyll, miss, then best you join him there. This here's a respectable house, always has been, and we don't accept unescorted females."

She forced herself to remain calm. "But I am not unescorted. These," she added, indicating Jonathan and Peter, "are my brothers."

The landlord's grunt told her all too succinctly his

opinion of schoolboy escorts. "Sorry, miss, but rules is rules. Ye'll need to find other accommoda—"

"Ah, Miss Pelham," said a deep, rather commanding voice, "how fortunate that I found you."

Charlotte turned at the sound of her name, but the only person she saw was the gray-eyed stranger, the driver of the Tilbury. He had obviously gone directly to the taproom, for he held a pewter tankard in his hand. At any other time, Charlotte would have been happy to be afforded a second look at such an attractive gentleman, but at the moment she wished he had not been a witness to her embarrassment.

Had he, too, known that she told a falsehood? Even though the ruse was absolutely necessary, she felt heat rush to her face just imagining what the stranger must be thinking of her.

When she had read the travel agency advertisement in the *Times*, offering sixty-five pounds for an experienced guide to lead a cross-country walking tour, Charlotte had seen an opportunity to establish herself in a career—one that would support her and allow her to pay her brother's tuition to Cambridge. Furthermore, it was a job she could do.

With her mother newly married to the vicar, Mr. Seth Williams, who had four children of his own to feed, Charlotte knew it was time she made her own way in the world. Though she had never tried to earn her living at the conventional female employments of teaching children or acting as some elderly lady's companion, Charlotte knew she was not temperamentally suited for such occupations. Furthermore, those positions often paid as little as twenty pounds per annum. Leading two-week tours, she might easily earn close to four hundred pounds from May through August, doing a job she loved.

For that reason, acting as a cross-country guide had seemed the perfect answer. She had known without asking, however, that a woman would never be accepted by the agency, no matter how skilled she might be. So, she had applied for the position as Charles Pelham, just until she proved herself to her employers.

Just the one little lie. Everything else she had said in her letters was true.

She had years of experience walking that particular route with her father, and she was an expert climber and camper. She was more than competent to lead a party of eight—with or without her two assistants—through the Lake District, over the Pennine Chain, and onward to the North York Moors. Furthermore, to ensure that she got the chance to show what she was capable of doing, she had promised the gentleman of Bonaventure Tours that if she did not arrive at Robin Hood's Bay within the scheduled fortnight, with at least five of her party pleased with their trip, she would forgo her fee as guide.

She had not, however, expected to meet with difficulties at the first inn, before the tour had even begun!

Mr. Harrison Montgomery had seen the young woman and the two lads in the inn yard. Now, as he watched the woman's dismay at the landlord's reception, Harrison smiled, for it was exactly the sort of opening he had hoped for.

After chasing the threesome for the past sixty miles, from Lancashire almost to the sea, he was tired, gritty eyed, and as thirsty as the dry, cracked earth of India just before the monsoon season. His purpose in going immediately to the taproom had been two-fold. First, he wished to soothe his parched throat with a tankard of ale, and second, he intended to intercept the young woman and the two lads before they went to their bedchambers. It was now or never, for if his information was correct, they meant to leave at first light the next day.

It had been easy enough for Harrison to hear what the woman said about an older brother, and it was equally easy to discern that every word she spoke was a fabrication. Obviously she had no experience at dissembling, for she did it badly.

Not that the foolish female should have been there in the first place. A tour guide, for heaven's sake. What lunacy!

Harrison bit back a swearword fit only for the ears of the rough sailors who had been his companions during his formative years aboard the East Indiaman. Accustomed to Eastern women—women who knew their place in a man's world and never overstepped those boundaries—he still could not believe this Englishwoman had taken it upon herself to lead a tour. And now it appeared she had lied to secure the position.

She should have been back in Lancashire, where she belonged, doing whatever the deuce the women of Burley did to occupy their time. A female had no business racketing about the north country, dragging two inexperienced youths in her wake. Especially when Harrison had every reason to believe that one of those lads was his own flesh and blood—Timmy, the half brother he had not seen in more than a dozen years!

Chapter Two

"Ah, Miss Pelham," Harrison said, stepping forward and making the woman a polite bow, "how fortunate that I found you. I have a message for you from your brother, Mr. Charles Pelham. I met him not ten miles back, and he asked me to offer you my services."

The lads stepped forward, as if to shield their "sister" from the advances of a stranger, but Miss Pelham stayed them by replying to Harrison. "A message from Charles?" she said, her voice none too steady. "Pray, sir, what had my brother to say?"

She had a head on her shoulders, Harrison would give her that, for she had not panicked at the landlord's refusal to house her, nor had she turned missish at being approached by a stranger. Of course, if she had not undertaken this idiotic scheme, assistance would not have been necessary. "Your brother asked me, ma'am, to give you five pounds, which you, in turn, are to give to the innkeeper as a token of Charles's appreciation for any inconvenience his delay may have caused."

While he spoke, he reached inside his coat and withdrew a Morocco leather pocketbook, removed a five-pound note, then held it not toward her but toward the innkeeper. As he suspected, the fellow made haste to claim the unexpected largesse. "And now, my good man, if you will be so good as to have someone show

Miss Pelham to her chamber, I am certain one of her *younger* brothers will be happy to sign the inn book."

Harrison wished to speak privately with the lads, to determine by a series of relevant questions which of the two was his own brother, and if he was any judge of the matter, they would speak more freely once the woman took herself off to her room. Once Miss Pelham was gone, he could invite the lads to join him in the taproom, and with any luck, it should not take him long to discover which of the youths was Timmy.

"Never mind," Miss Pelham said, dashing Harrison's plans by turning once again to the counter and acting for all the world as though she had not been within a hairbreadth of being tossed out on her ear. "I will sign for all three of us."

She signed quickly, then held out her hand for the two keys the landlord removed from the wall pegs behind him.

Managing female! Could she not see that she was not wanted? No matter. Harrison had dealt with too many cutthroats in his lifetime to let a slip of a girl deter him from his path.

Not that she was a "slip" exactly. True, the figure beneath the sensible russet brown traveling dress and the Devonshire brown pelisse appeared slender enough and reasonably curvaceous, but unless Harrison missed his guess, Miss Charlotte Pelham was one of those most pathetic of creatures—a female who wished to be a male. He would wager his last groat that her naked form would be firm and taut as a young boy's. Why, she might even have developed a bit of musculature.

For Harrison, who liked his women soft to the touch and very feminine, the mere notion of muscles on a female gave him a bad taste in his mouth. He took a deep swallow of his ale just to cleanse his palate.

Athletic females! There should be a law against such a travesty of nature!

At just that moment, Miss Pelham surprised him by coming toward him, a conspiratorial smile on her lips. The smile revealed the merest hint of a dimple in her right cheek and lit those dark brown eyes, and for just a moment Harrison found his attention caught by an unexpectedly pretty face.

"Sir," she said sotto voce, "I cannot thank you enough for your assistance. And if I had an older brother, which, as you must know, I do not, I am persuaded he would thank you as well."

Harrison was about to voice the expected platitude about having been happy to be of service, when the woman turned to her *brothers*, raising her voice once again. "Peter, Jonathan," she said, pitching one of the keys to the lad she called Jonathan. "You both know what you are to do. When your tasks are completed, I will meet you back down here for supper."

Peter? Jonathan? The solicitor had informed Harrison that his half brother's name had been changed eleven years ago, at the time of the formal adoption, but somehow Harrison had expected the lad to still answer to Timmy.

"Come, sir," Miss Pelham said, as though she was accustomed to giving orders and having them obeyed. "Let us adjourn to the common room, where we will not be overheard."

She turned then, and preceded him into the room, not stopping until she was beside the unlit fireplace. Setting his tankard on a piecrust table nearby, Harrison followed her lead, though it went ill with him to do so. Had the woman no notion of proper feminine behavior?

"Now," she said, "we can speak without being

overheard, and I can repay the five pounds you were so kind as to bestow upon the landlord."

"That is not at all necessary, ma'am. Surely one of your brothers can return the money. In fact, I had meant to ask the lads if they would join me later for a tankard of mein host's excellent home brew."

"Oh, no thank you, sir. My brothers are far too busy for socializing. They have much to do in preparation for our departure at first light tomorrow. As I am to lead a cross-country walking tour, you will understand that I, too, am pressed for time. Therefore, if you will allow me . . ." Her voice trailed off as she dug into the reticule that hung from her wrist.

Deuce take it! Harrison had not come all this way merely to be dismissed by the likes of Miss Charlotte Pelham. He must have an opportunity to speak with the lads, and the matter was much too important to be rushed. One could not merely grab a young man by the arm and blurt out, "Excuse me, but are you my brother? You are? Excellent. Happy to have found you at last. For now, though, have a pleasant journey, and I will see you in a fortnight, when this blasted walking tour is completed."

Not bloody likely!

Frustrated almost beyond endurance, Harrison only just controlled his desire to warm the air with a few well-chosen curses. He had spent eight years at sea, then another four years with the East India Company, all with only one objective in mind—to amass enough money to return to England to find his brother. Now, when he had funds enough to last him through a dozen lifetimes, Harrison had come home only to discover obstacles at every turn.

The first of those obstacles had resulted from his own foolish blunder. Like the veriest Johnny Raw, he had placed an advertisement in the London papers, offering a handsome reward for information concerning the whereabouts of his brother. Unfortunately, Harrison's reputation as a wealthy India nabob spread through the town like a wind-driven fire, and within a matter of days, dozens of imposters had sought him out, each of them claiming to be his long-lost brother.

The last straw had come in the form of a potbellied individual who could not have been a day under forty. After tossing the yahoo out on his ear, Harrison had quit his suite of rooms at Pulteney's Hotel and turned the entire matter over to the Bow Street Runners hired by his solicitor.

The gist of what the runners had learned was that after the death of Thomas James, Harrison's stepfather and Timmy's real father, the three-year-old had been passed from one member of the James family to another. Obviously, those relatives had found a young boy too much to handle, especially once his mother's scant fortune had been spent, and Timmy had become a ward of the court.

Finally, at the age of four, the little boy had been formally adopted by a family named Newsome—a family thought to reside in Lancashire. Or so the runners had been told.

Actually, the adoption was merely hearsay, for there was no tangible proof. The paper trail had been lost somewhere between Chancery Court and the offices where adoption information was filed.

One of the Lord Chancellor's clerks swore to the runners that he remembered the case, and based on his testimony alone, Harrison had sped to Lancashire, to the village of Burley. Of course, he had no guarantee that the clerk's memory was not a hoax to gain the promised reward money, so Harrison had promised himself he would proceed cautiously, taking nothing for granted.

He had planned to spend some time in Burley—

days, even weeks if necessary—where he might discover more about the Newsome family and the boy they called their son. With little to go on other than his own memories of the brother he had not seen since the child was three, Harrison had hoped he would recognize familiar traits in the boy.

When he arrived in Burley, however, he found the squire and Mrs. Newsome gone to Bath. According to the near imbecile who served as ostler at the small inn, the Newsomes' son was on his way to St. Bee's Head to join a walking tour. "Not two hours past," he added, "I seen 'im and Master Pelham boarding t'stagecoach to Cumbria, them and Miss Charlotte Pelham."

In his frustration at being thwarted once again, coupled with his eagerness to see if he could catch up with the stagecoach, Harrison had not thought to ask the ostler the Newsome lad's name. Now, what was he to do? The boys looked enough alike to actually be Miss Pelham's brothers, and Harrison could not ask too many questions without raising suspicion about his own identity.

Having learned from his London experience, he did not want anyone to guess that he was what the *ton* called a nabob, especially when he had no way of knowing if Timmy even wished to be reunited with an older brother who had disappeared from his life twelve years ago. If Timmy did not wish it, Harrison certainly did not want a reunion, especially if it was based solely upon the boy's desire to share his wealth.

What Harrison needed was time. Unfortunately, since the walking party was scheduled to leave early tomorrow, what little time he had was running out.

While Miss Pelham was still digging in her reticule for the five-pound note to repay him, Harrison came to a decision. Knowing it was the only one way to gain the time he needed, he spoke before he had an opportunity to change his mind. "Miss Pelham, I wish to join your tour."

She looked up at him, surprise writ plainly on her face. "Pardon me?"

"Your cross-country walking tour. I wish to take part." Again he withdrew the Morocco leather pocketbook. "If you will tell me the charge, I am prepared to pay—"

"I am sorry," Miss Pelham said, her tone tinged with sympathy, "but I am afraid that is not possible. Payment is arranged through the London travel service, Bonaventure Tours. Besides, we already have eight people, which for our first time out is considered a full complement."

"Nonsense, madam. What difference can one more person make?"

"To me," she replied, a touch of coolness replacing the previous sympathy, "no difference whatever. But, as I said, Bonaventure set the rules, and as their employee, I do not feel it proper for me to make unauthorized changes."

"You are the guide, madam. You can make your own rules."

"No," she said quietly, "I cannot. Now, please, let that be an end to it."

"So," he said, "let me see if I have this correctly. You can lie to your employer, as well as to the people on the tour, about there being a Mr. Charles Pelham, but you cannot change one small rule?"

"Well, I—"

"How like a female to enact a needlessly foolish demonstration of straining gnats and swallowing camels."

She stiffened, then drew breath as though intending to give him a piece of her mind. Obviously thinking better of whatever she had meant to say, she caught

her bottom lip between her teeth, as if to force herself
to remain silent. The technique proved successful, for
without further comment, she returned her attention
to the reticule, though Harrison was unsure how
much of her controlled anger was an act put on for
his benefit. For all he knew, she was being difficult
merely to raise the price of the tour so she might line
her own pockets with the overflow.

So be it! He had not spent twelve years in the
Orient for nothing; he knew when someone else held
all the bargaining chips, and in this instance haggling
over a few pounds was the last thing he wished to
do. He had lots of money; what he needed was time
in which to become reacquainted with his brother.

Holding the Morocco pocketbook in front of him,
Harrison slipped the thick stack of pound notes out
just far enough for the woman to get a good look.
"Naturally, ma'am, since I am late joining the group,
I expect to pay extra."

Continuing as he had done many times over the
years, when a bit of palm greasing was called for, he
added, "And, of course, there is your own inconvenience to be considered. Merely advise me what you
consider to be fair, and I will—"

"Sir!"

Her tone was now decidedly frosty, and from the
color creeping up her face, Harrison realized too late
that he had blundered.

"As I said before, sir, the travel service set the limit
for the tour, and I have no authority to change that
number. So, if you will excuse me, I really must be
going."

No stranger to the need for desperate measures,
Harrison raised his voice, speaking so the innkeeper
could not avoid hearing him. "But you do not understand, Miss Pelham. When I met your brother—
Charles, I believe he said his name was—he accepted

me as one of the party. Surely, as the official tour guide, *Mr.* Pelham's word on such matters is final."

If looks could kill, Harrison would have fallen to the floor on the instant, for Miss Charlotte Pelham's angry eyes shot at least a dozen arrows at him, each aimed directly at his heart. "Sir," she muttered, the word barely audible, "this is . . . is *blackmail*."

"Tsk, tsk, madam. Such an unpleasant word. In the Orient, this is considered nothing more than friendly bargaining."

Her back went ramrod straight. "I know nothing of the Orient, nor what passes for acceptable behavior among its inhabitants. However, in this country, when one person places undue pressure upon another, it is not called bargaining. It is called blackmail, pure and simple."

"Now, there, madam, is the basic flaw in your logic, for in my experience, life is seldom pure and it is never simple."

When she made as if to brush past him, Harrison caught her by the wrist, obliging her to remain or risk causing a scene. "The fact is," he said, relaxing his fingers yet not letting her go, "though I am loath to bring this to your attention, if I *truly* wished to exert 'undue pressure,' as you called it, I could do so quite easily. I could merely seek out my fellow ramblers and inquire if they are aware that Mr. Charles Pelham is nothing more than a figment of the actual guide's imagination."

Her face lost all color.

"People have so many prejudices," he continued softly, "that one wonders how many of the party would refuse to embark on such a long journey if they knew their leader was, in fact, a young female who—"

"Bargain!" she said, albeit through clenched teeth. Harrison released her wrist and bowed slightly.

"Madam, I cannot thank you enough for your kindness in allowing me to—"

"Spare me your sarcasm. Instead, listen carefully, for I will have you understand one thing."

"And that is?"

"As you pointed out, I *am* the guide, and as such, I am prepared to make every allowance for the lack of skills in the original eight members of the party. However, I will make no allowances for you. Furthermore, when there is more than one possible route to our day's destination, I mean to take a vote to see just how adventurous the members of the group wish to be."

"Very democratic of you, Miss Pel—"

"At no time, sir, will you be allowed to participate in those group discussions. There will be eight votes and eight only. And if you should lag behind, no matter what the reason, I will leave you. And that, Mr. Blackmailer, is a promise."

The woman had spunk; he would give her that.

This time, she did brush past him, her clear intention to put as much distance between them as possible, and as Harrison turned to watch her walk away, her nose in the air as though she passed some sort of vermin on the road, some imp inside him prompted him to tease her a bit. Feigning shock, he said, "You would actually leave me in the wilderness? Without a guide? Alone and friendless?"

She had reached the stairs that led to the upper floors, but at his question, she turned back. "As for your being friendless, one might be forgiven for assuming that such a circumstance owes much to your way of doing business."

Score a second point to her! "But, ma'am, what if I am seriously injured? Would you still leave me? Only consider, if you will, how even the most experienced

person might accidentally lose his footing and plunge
down the side of a mountain.''

A smile curled the corners of her lips. Rather pretty
lips, Harrison noticed. They were full and slightly
pink, a perfect complement to her smooth, ivory skin.
"Hmm," she said. "A plunge down the mountain-
side. Now there is an interesting thought." The smile
vanished. "Take a bit of advice, sir. Any more of
your brand of bargaining, and such a plunge will be
no accident."

"Why, madam. What can you mean?"

"I mean I will push you myself! Then, I *will* leave
you. Just you and the buzzards."

The sound of the detestable man's laughter had
followed Charlotte all the way up the stairs, and she
was still fuming when the entire party met at three
o'clock that afternoon for their first tea together. The
latest addition to their ranks was there, smiling and
making himself agreeable to his new acquaintances.
Obviously a scoundrel, he possessed neither shame
nor scruples, and Charlotte did her best to ignore
him.

How, she wondered, could she have ever thought
him the man of her dreams!

What a joke on her, to be so misled by a handsome
face and physique. And how lowering to realize that
she was no better than those idiotic gentlemen who
chose to wed a female for her looks alone, unmindful
of her intelligence or lack thereof. Charlotte had expected this trip to be a learning experience, but she
could never have guessed the full extent of the
lessons.

Unable to swallow more than a few bites of her
food, she rose and tapped her knife against her glass
to gain everyone's attention. Each of the original

eight had received instructions by post, containing a
list of appropriate shoes and clothing and the ap-
proximate route they would take, but Charlotte had
prepared a list of further instructions.

"Bonaventure Tours," she began, just a bit nervous
at speaking in public, "has supplied bedrolls, haversacks, rain gear, and water flasks. Each person will
carry his or her own haversack, containing the day's
noon meal, the water flask, and the rain gear. At
some time during the second week, weather permit-
ting, those who enjoy that sort of thing will have an
opportunity to sleep out-of-doors."

A murmur went through the group, and Charlotte
waited until she had everyone's attention once again.
"Naturally, no one is obliged to camp out. Arrange-
ments have been made at inns along the way, for all
fourteen evenings. A wagon, driven by one of my
brothers, will transport the luggage to and from each
day's inn. As well, there is room on the wagon for
two passengers, should anyone find themselves in
need of rest, or if they begin to feel unwell."

Without meaning to, Charlotte caught sight of Mr.
Harrison Montgomery, and remembering her threat
to push him off the side of a mountain, she felt herself blush. He must have read her thoughts, for he
lifted his sherry glass as if toasting her.

While he pressed the crystal to his lips and sipped
slowly of the amber-colored contents, Charlotte
found herself hoping he would choke. When he was
not so obliging, she returned her attention to the
other eight members of the party. "Are there any
questions?"

One gentleman stood. In his mid-fifties, and of medium height and build, he sported a rather impressive snow-white mustache—a mustache so thick it
covered his entire upper lip, and so long the left and
right points reached to his jawbone. Standing uncom-

monly erect, as if on parade, he looked every inch the military man. Making a calculated guess, Charlotte said, "Yes, Colonel Fitzgibbon?"

The military gentleman showed no surprise at being instantly recognized. In fact, he seemed to take it as his due. "I wondered, Miss Pelham, when we might expect to meet our guide, Mr. Charles Pelham?"

"Tomorrow," she replied, swallowing a sizeable lump in her throat, "at Ambleside. Meanwhile, Colonel, I, er, think it time we all introduced ourselves. My name you already know, and those are my brothers, Jonathan and Peter."

"And I," said a rather imperious grande dame, "am Julia Griswall."

Charlotte smiled at the lady, who wore a sensible plum-colored traveling costume, and whose salt-and-pepper hair was arranged in no-nonsense braids that circled the top of her head like a tiara. "A pleasure to have you with us, Lady Griswall."

Another murmur went through the group at the unexpected presence of one of the nobility. Charlotte, too, had experienced some misgivings about such a personage, but from the looks of her, her ladyship was at least forty years old and no hothouse plant.

Unfortunately, the same could not be said for the other female in the group. The new Mrs. Stephen Richardson and her husband were finishing up their wedding trip by returning to Whitby, Yorkshire, in company with the walking tour. Unless Charlotte missed her guess, Dora Richardson was not a day above eighteen, and if her blond curls and dainty pink silk frock were anything to go by, she was most definitely a delicate flower.

What in heaven's name had possessed her husband, a slender young gentleman who could not have been more than one-and-twenty, to undertake such a trip with his bride? If those two were still with the party at the end of the fourteen days, Charlotte would eat her best bonnet!

She did a quick calculation. To earn her share of the profits, she must arrive in Robin's Hood Bay with at least five paying customers. As she looked at the young newlyweds, her only question was not *if* they would drop out, but how soon.

Suddenly realizing what she was doing, Charlotte took herself to task for making yet another judgment based on a person's exterior. She closed her eyes, doubly ashamed of herself for having been guilty of this particular demonstration of prejudice.

Heaven help her, for she was no better than the rest of society, those who judged all females on the basis of their gender alone, without ever giving them an opportunity to show what was in their hearts and in their minds. How were females ever to gain any sort of equality in this world, if even the members of their own sex judged them on sight to be substandard?

Warning herself against any further snap judgments, yet grateful to the powers that be that she had a ninth traveler in case anyone—male or female— dropped out along the way, Charlotte opened her eyes. As luck would have it, her gaze collided again with that of the ninth man himself, Mr. Harrison Montgomery, who wore a satisfied smile on his face.

Drat the man! He knew exactly what she was thinking, and there was nothing she could do about it. "Bargain," he mouthed silently.

Suppressing a desire to go over and box the lout's ears, Charlotte turned away slowly, giving her attention to the remainder of the party, who were following the colonel's lead by standing to introduce themselves. At the moment, Mr. Andrew Vinton, a London solicitor in his mid-twenties, explained to the interested gathering that he was traveling with his younger brother, Mr. Lawrence Vinton, who was taking a short rest from his studies at Oxford. As for that young worthy, after turning several shades of red, he contented himself with rising and making a polite bow before resuming his seat.

The next gentleman to stand was Mr. Russell Thorne. "My home," he added rather shyly, "is in West Sussex, where I reside most of the year." The blond gentleman was about thirty-five, and though probably no more than five-foot-seven, and rather slender, he appeared to be quite fit. His confession that he was both a birder and a seasoned climber came as no surprise to Charlotte, and she was glad to know that at least one of the group would not need to be watched.

The final member of the party to introduce himself was Mr. Wilfred Bryce. Fully six feet tall, and in his early thirties, his reddish brown hair and small, muddy green eyes put Charlotte in mind of a fox. Worse yet, the smile seemed never to leave Mr. Bryce's thin lips, and he saw fit to apologize to one and all for being nothing more than a poor clerk on holiday, and a complete novice at cross-country walking. "But I'll try my best not to delay them as are more seasoned walkers."

Charlotte drew breath to tell him that there were no requirements as to skill, when he ruined her good intentions by turning to Lady Griswall and bowing at the waist. "And I apologize especially to your ladyship, who is, I make no doubt, accustomed to the most exalted company. Rest assured, ma'am, that Wilfred Bryce knows his place, and after this moment I mean to speak only when spoken to."

Though Charlotte cautioned herself not to judge the man too severely, the task was not easy, for with every word that issued from his mouth, he branded himself a toadeater of the first order.

That evening, just after Charlotte blew out her bedside candle in hopes of getting a few hours sleep, she asked her Heavenly Father for His assistance. "I never expected such a diverse group, and if I am to prove capable of the task I set myself as their guide, I may have need of a bit of divine intervention."

In closing, she begged the Lord's blessings upon her brother, her mother, her mother's new husband, and the vicar's four small children. Before she finished her prayers, however, she was overcome by a most irreverent thought, one that prompted an unholy giggle to pass her lips. "And," she added, confident that the Omniscient One would know she was in jest, "if during the coming fortnight, the occasion should arise that I push Mr. Harrison Montgomery off some mountain, please let him have the good grace to take the toadying Mr. Bryce over the side with him."

Chapter Three

Monday morning was everything Charlotte could have hoped for. The day was warm and sunny, and all nine members of the party were below stairs when she arrived, ready and willing to begin their walking tour.

Except for Mr. Harrison Montgomery, who wore a corbeau green coat, dark green breeches, top boots, and a curly brim beaver—perfectly acceptable clothing for a gentleman on a relaxing holiday in the country—the men all wore clothing suitable for serious walking. To a man, they were outfitted in loose sporting jackets, heavy walking or spit boots, slouch hats, and haversacks. As for the ladies, Charlotte was pleased to see that Dora Richardson had donned a dark blue habit and stout walking boots.

Charlotte, too, wore a riding habit, and though the bronze green faille with the bronze trim had been shortened to her ankles, to make walking that much easier, she was consumed with jealousy once she spied Lady Griswall's ensemble. Her ladyship, no newcomer to long-distance rambling, wore a damson brown skirt whose fullness had been divided in the middle to form a barely discernible breecheslike garment.

Apparently, Dora Richardson had already noticed the frock and marveled over its suitability, for her ladyship was showing the girl the leather sewn into the hem of the skirt, leather that could be gathered close around each ankle and tied should the wearer wish to try her skill at rock climbing. Vowing to have such a garment made for herself the instant the trip was completed, Charlotte declared the walk begun and bid them all follow her.

The morning's ramble led them within sight of Great Gable, and though that brooding fell was not on their list of stops, it being far too early in the trip to test the travelers overmuch, Charlotte paused for several minutes to marvel at the giant hill's snow-covered beauty. Such grandeur deserved more time for contemplation; unfortunately, to give every scenic view suitable reverence would require double the fortnight allotted for the trip. There would be fells enough in the coming days; for now, the dales were their objective, so they moved on.

As they headed south, over one of the well-blazed paths to Ambleside, Charlotte spent time with each member of the party, attempting to form an early opinion of each person's stamina. To her relief, all but the toadeating Mr. Bryce appeared to know what they were about.

Wilfred Bryce had already stumbled twice, and when he apologized for what must have been the tenth time for his clumsiness, Colonel Fitzgibbon advised him to put a sock in it! "Far better to be silent and pass for a fool," the colonel informed him, "than to be constantly opening your mummer and proving the point beyond all doubt."

At that moment, Charlotte had the misfortune to be walking behind the colonel and just ahead of Harrison Montgomery, and when she could not contain her laughter at the colonel's rather ruthless instruction, Mr. Montgomery took the opportunity to step up beside her. "Some advice," he said, keeping his voice low enough so he was not overheard, "should be heeded by both the giver and the receiver."

She had been avoiding "The Blackmailer" all morning, but now she was far too curious as to what he meant to give him the cut direct. Tipping her head slightly so she could look up at the tall man, she asked him to what he referred.

"Are you familiar with Shakespeare's *Hamlet*, Miss Pelham?"

"Of course," she replied, none too affably. Did the man think her some illiterate bumpkin? "During my sixth year at the Manchester Female Academy, I portrayed Ophelia in the closing-week festivities." *There! That will show him!*

"Ophelia?" he asked, not even bothering to hide his amused grin. "Somehow, Miss Pelham, I would have expected you to try for the part of Hamlet."

She *had* tried out for the lead part, but she would not give this smiling oaf the satisfaction of knowing it! Nor would she lower herself to inform him that she had been much better suited to the part of the melancholy Dane, being taller and far more proficient at the required swordplay than her classmate, Lady Anne Worthing. Since Lady Anne was the academy's star boarder, the lead role had been hers for the asking, but Charlotte kept all that information to herself.

"Allow me to inform you, sir, that I was an excellent Ophelia."

"Then you will be familiar with the poor lady's father, and understand when I tell you that after an evening in Colonel Fitzgibbon's company, I had nightmares in which I was pursued relentlessly by Polonius."

Remembering Ophelia's father, who gave his son Laertes pages and pages' worth of unsolicited advice, Charlotte was obliged to smother another laugh. "Never

tell me, sir, that our military friend is given to platitudes."

"His store, I fear, is inexhaustible."

"Oh, no," she said, this time laughing aloud.

Mr. Montgomery smiled, revealing even, white
teeth, and causing Charlotte to admit, albeit grudg-
ingly, that he was a very handsome man.

Because she had walked for several minutes with
each of the other members of the party, she could
not desert Mr. Montgomery so quickly without appearing to deny him his money's worth of the
guide's attention. For that reason, they walked
abreast for about a mile. During that mile, she attempted to put him from her mind, concentrating
instead upon the beautiful weather and the spectacular scenery of the Lake District.

"A marvelous day," he offered after several minutes of silence. "I have been away from England
since I was a lad of fifteen, when I went to sea, but
if I remember correctly, such days as this are not to
be counted upon."

He went to sea at fifteen?

Having never agreed with the practice of sending
young boys to sea, where they reputedly endured
all manner of hardships, Charlotte knew a moment's
sympathy for the lad he used to be. Though she had
vowed to treat Mr. Montgomery with reserve, in payment for his having blackmailed his way into the
group, her compassion got the better of her. "Your
memory has not played you false," she said, speaking kindly. "The weather, or rather the fickleness of
the weather, is the primary reason this debut tour
travels from west to east. Hopefully, when the wind
and rain come, as they most certainly will, they will
be at our backs."

Harrison, having spent eight years at sea, four of
them as captain of his own Indiaman, could have

told her a thing or two about changeable weather. He said nothing, however, for the young lady was obviously attempting to put aside her previous animosity, at least for the moment, and he was enjoying her company. It had been years since he had been in company with a young Englishwoman, and after the Eastern women of his acquaintance—females who invariably let the man do most of the talking—it was refreshing to converse with a member of the fair sex who showed him not the least deference.

As well, he found it surprisingly pleasant to walk with a woman who did not need to be shielded from every rise and dip in the path. Not having to look out for her welfare every minute allowed Harrison to enjoy the scenery and to walk at his own pace. In fact, once or twice he found himself obliged to increase his own speed to keep up with her!

As he had suspected, Miss Pelham was uncommonly fit for a female, much more so than the young bride in blue or Lady Griswall, who were showing themselves to be better than average walkers. Of course, it was early yet to draw any permanent conclusions, but if the ersatz Charles continued in this manner, Harrison would be obliged to revise his opinion of her ability to guide the group.

She had certainly chosen the perfect route for their initial walk, for this morning's ramble had been invigorating without being the least bit taxing. As well, since the path they had followed for the past hour tended toward an easy, downward slope, it offered an unobstructed view of a gentler version of the Lakeland scenery, with stone walls and colorful cottages by the scores. Fluffy white sheep grazed behind the walls, and in one of the many small green fields that were dotted with rocky outcrops, Harrison spotted a doe and her fawn roaming about in search of tasty morsels.

He had forgotten just how lovely and green his homeland could be, and he was lost in admiration of the countryside, dressed as it was in white-flowering rowans and wild cherry trees, when Miss Pelham asked him how he came to go to sea at such a tender age.

"I was given no choice in the matter."

He made his answer brief and just terse enough to discourage further conversation along that line. He did not wish to ruin his pleasure in the morning with thoughts of his stepfather, whose idea it had been to send Harrison from his home.

"Oh," she said. "I . . . I see."

Of course she did not see. How could she? How could anyone understand unless they, too, had been subjected to the whims of a tyrant like his stepfather? A thoroughly mean-spirited man, Thomas James had hated sharing his meek, obedient wife and his three-year-old son with a youth who was, in his words, "another man's get."

Harrison glanced away, but when he turned back, Miss Pelham's intelligent, dark brown eyes were fixed upon him, as if she attempted to discover for herself the story he did not wish to tell.

"My guardian thought I would be well suited to the seaman's life," he said rather sharply, "so the day I turned fifteen, he took me to Bristol and handed me over to the captain of an Indiaman. I was tall for my age, so the captain asked no questions." Harrison did not look at her to see her reaction, and he was more than thankful that she asked no more questions.

Before long, the path became steeper, zigzagging past a fast-moving stream that tumbled down to a waterfall—a waterfall that apparently fed the pretty blue lake Harrison saw some two hundred yards farther down.

"In this area," Miss Pelham said, purposefully introducing a new subject by motioning toward the stream that was progressing apace toward the steep, noisy fall, "the streams are called becks, or ghylls, and a waterfall is called a force."

"And what of the lake?" he asked, happy to pursue this harmless topic. "Have I a new name to learn there as well?"

"But of course," she replied, "for it is called a tarn."

As the path became steeper, their pace picked up, making further conversation impossible. Soon the path grew narrower as well, with a good twenty-foot drop-off to their right, so Harrison allowed Miss Pelham to step in front of him, for safety's sake. She had only just moved forward when he heard a shout close behind him. An instant later, the bumble-footed Mr. Bryce crashed against Harrison's back with tremendous force, obliging him to use all his strength to brace himself, thereby avoiding a catastrophe.

Fortunately for all concerned, Harrison was a large man, accustomed to keeping his balance aboard a rocking ship, and he managed to stop Bryce's descent without any harm to himself. Had the fellow collided with a smaller man, or a female, that person might well have suffered a nasty fall down the twenty-foot drop. As it was, Harrison had spared a second to push Miss Pelham to the left, just in case he lost his footing.

"A thousand apologies," Bryce said, once he picked himself up off the ground. "Miss Pelham?" he called. "Are you all right?"

"Of course she is not all right!" Harrison put his hands beneath her elbows and lifted her to her feet. "How could she be, when I was obliged to knock her to the ground?"

"For which," she said rather breathlessly, "I am most sincerely grateful."

Harrison had expected tears, if not a fit of the va-
pors, either of which he would have deemed understandable under the circumstances. What he got for
his rough handling of her was a tremulous smile that
hit him solidly in his solar plexus, the blow far more
unsettling than the one he had received from that
bumbling oaf who remained behind him, still uttering apologies and excuses.

"How can I thank you," she said softly, looking
directly into his eyes, "for your quick thinking?"

As Harrison stood there, holding Miss Pelham by
her elbows, her slightly unsteady hands resting on
his forearms and her face turned up to his, he wondered how he had failed to notice before what lovely
skin she had. It was soft and smooth, with the pearly
sheen of pure silk, and while he stared at her, that skin
mere inches away, he was overcome with the strongest
desire to brush his fingers along the gentle contour
of her jaw to see if her complexion was as silken as
it appeared.

"Ma'am!" Wilfred Bryce said, pushing his way
past Harrison so he could look the lady in the face.
"I cannot think how this happened. Pray forgive
my ineptitude."

"Think nothing of it," she replied politely, "for
anyone might stumble on such a path as this."

Harrison was not so polite. In fact, if Miss Pelham
had not been present, he might have followed his
inclination and caught Bryce by the collar, giving him
a good shake. "In the future," he said rather sharply,
"watch your step. A second earlier and you might
have caused a serious injury."

"For which, sir and ma'am, I would never have
forgiven myself."

Harrison made no reply, for something had him
puzzled. Not too long ago Bryce had been up front,

walking with Colonel Fitzgibbon. How the deuce had the fellow managed to get behind them?

"It may take you a few days to feel your walking limbs beneath you," Miss Pelham said. "In the meantime, Mr. Bryce, it would be best if you did not attempt to travel faster than is necessary."

She motioned Harrison ahead of them, and when the path widened once again to accommodate two abreast, Miss Pelham walked beside the clerk. For the remainder of the distance to the lake, where they were to stop for their noonday rest, she talked with Bryce, from time to time offering him encouragement.

In Harrison's estimation, she was behaving far more amiably than the fellow deserved, a fact that probably spoke well for her character. As for himself, Harrison had no illusions whatsoever about his own character, for he had taken Wilfred Bryce in almost instant dislike. For some reason—a reason that had nothing to do with the man's looks or his demeanor— Bryce reminded Harrison of his stepfather.

Not at all happy to be reminded once again of Thomas James, Harrison directed his thoughts toward his half brother and the two boys who posed as Miss Pelham's brothers.

The youth who called himself Jonathan Pelham had set out quite early that morning, together with Lady Griswall's maid, driving the cumbersome luggage wagon to the Ghyll Inn in Ambleside—the inn where the spurious Mr. Charles Pelham was reputed to be waiting. Not wanting to miss any opportunity to garner possible information, Harrison had bid his servant, Benizur, drive the Tilbury, following close behind the wagon. Once the vehicles reached the inn, Benizur was to see if he could strike up a conversation with the lad, hopefully to trip him up and get him to reveal which one of the two "brothers" was not actually a member of the Pelham family.

Benizur had a knack for uncovering information others hoped to keep secret, and many times over the past twelve years Harrison had depended upon the smallish man, a native of India, to be his second pair of eyes and ears.

Several months after Harrison came aboard his first Indiaman, Benizur and four of his countrymen were shanghaied from the docks of Bombay to fill the places of sailors who had jumped ship. Due to his size, Benizur was made cabin boy, and because he and Harrison were of a similar age and both were miserable at sea, they had struck up a friendship.

Later, when a French privateer shot the Indiaman out from under them and they were obliged to abandon ship, Harrison had saved the much smaller Benizur from drowning by dragging him aboard a piece of floating hull. Since that time, Benizur had remained by Harrison's side, his goal to repay the debt he felt he owed for his life.

Naturally, Harrison did not feel that any repayment was necessary, and he looked up on Benizur as more loyal friend than servant. Still, he was happy to know that the inscrutable Indian was doing his part to help him find his brother, especially since Harrison had not come within fifty feet of the other lad during the entire morning. Hopefully, he would have better luck once they reached the lake and stopped for their noon meal.

Charlotte was more than happy when they finally reached the pretty blue lake, the first of many they would see in the next few days. The incident earlier had unnerved her more than she wished to admit, firstly because she had narrowly escaped a nasty fall—a fall that might well have rendered her incapable of continuing the tour—and secondly because she was now in Mr. Harrison Montgomery's debt.

She did not wish to be beholden to him. He had forced his way into the group by using totally unscrupulous tactics, and she did not wish to forget that fact. What difference did it make if his quick actions had spared her a painful fall? None. Not the slightest difference. Nor did it matter in the least that when he set her on her feet, his strong hands firmly beneath her elbows, she had felt a delicious tingle all the way to her toes. As for those mysterious gray eyes that seemed to look deep within her soul—well, anyone might have gray eyes!

He was still an unprincipled person, not to mention one who had appeared as if from nowhere—a stranger with who-knew-how-many crimes and indiscretions in his past—and she had no intention of falling under his spell.

Of course, she'd had no intention of spending half an hour in company with Wilfred Bryce either, but that was what had transpired. She had fallen into step with Bryce, wishing only to avoid further conversation with Harrison Montgomery. Unfortunately, her wish had been granted with a vengeance! The gray-eyed blackmailer had walked on ahead, joining Colonel Fitzgibbon without so much as a backward glance in Charlotte's direction, while she had spent the next thirty minutes with the toadeating clerk.

One half hour. Who would have thought it could seem like a month?

Charlotte had been taxed almost beyond endurance, especially when Bryce forsook his obsequiousness in favor of asking her repeated questions about their missing tour guide. No matter how she tried to turn the conversation, the fellow always returned to the subject of Charles.

Thankfully, the path finally ended, and once Charlotte escaped from the clerk, giving as her excuse her
need to join the rest of the party, she hurried across
the idyllic bit of greensward that stretched the thirty
yards or so to the water's edge. The small lake was
a perfect mirror for the clear, cloudless sky, with the
peaceful beauty of the water further enhanced by the
sight of at least a dozen willow trees, their feathery
green leaves swaying in the gentle breeze, adding
their calming magic to that of the sky.

Charlotte stopped for a moment, allowing the harmony of her surroundings to wash over her, restor-
ing her to her usual equilibrium. The lake was
neither large enough nor grand enough to attract the
usual crowd of Lakeland visitors, so the small band
of ramblers had the entire area to themselves. As if
in deference to nature's gift, they were all, like her,
communing silently.

"My sympathies lie with poor Mr. Charles Pelham," Lady Griswall said quietly, "for he is missing
all this."

Charlotte had been too caught up in the view to
notice the lady's arrival, but at the mention of the ersatz
Charles, she was once again on her mettle. Fortunately, one look at the serene expression on Lady
Griswall's rather plain face was enough to convince
Charlotte that the lady's remark held no hidden
meaning. " 'Tis a most pleasing spot, ma'am."

"How true. I love these quiet, out-of-the-way
places. Especially after the busy racketing about of
the season."

"You were recently in town, ma'am?"

The lady nodded. "For the better part of two
months. My late husband's niece had her come-out,
and my sister-in-law, Lady Barrett, would not be
satisfied until I promised to spend several weeks as
her guest."

From the tone of her voice, it was apparent Lady Griswall had found the prospect of a few weeks in town far from pleasing. At a loss as to what she should say, Charlotte chose to remark on the invitation itself. "How nice, ma'am, that your sister-in-law was desirous of your company."

"Humph," her ladyship replied. "I fear the pleasure of my company was not nearly so valuable to Lady Barrett as was my influence with the patronesses of Almack's. Or one patroness in particular, Mrs. Drummond-Burrell."

Though Charlotte had never had a London season—her late father's small inheritance not allowing for trips to town—she knew all about Almack's, that holiest of holies, and the importance of a voucher for the Wednesday evening subscription balls. Any young lady desirous of taking her place among the *ton* must be seen at Almack's, and to receive one of the coveted vouchers, the young lady must first pass the rigorous standards set by the "Magnificent Seven." Of those seven ladies who presided over Almack's, none was more to be feared than the disdainful, toplofty Clementina Drummond-Burrell.

"Clementina's father, Lord Perth, and my own dear papa were boyhood friends," Lady Griswall said, "and though I am a few years older than Clementina, we became friends. And are friends still, I am happy to say."

As interested as the next female in the *on-dits* of society, Charlotte said, "And your niece received her voucher?"

"What?" her ladyship asked, her attention caught by the laughter of Mr. Harrison Montgomery, who had struck up a conversation with the young newlyweds. "Oh, yes, she got the voucher, after which I—having done my part—claimed that I was coming down with a putrid sore throat so I might take myself off. I had seen the advertisement in the paper for this walking tour, and though I do not usually travel with strangers, I knew a good ramble was just the thing to blow the staleness of too many London parties from my head."

"And is it working, ma'am?"

Lady Griswall did not answer the question, for once again her attention had been claimed by Mr. Montgomery, who had taken his leave of the Richardsons, and was now walking rather purposefully toward Peter, who stood at the water's edge, skipping stones across the surface of the lake. "Pray," she said, "what is Mr. Montgomery up to now?"

Surprised by the question, especially the last part of it, Charlotte said, "Now? Forgive me, ma'am, but do you know Mr. Mont—"

"Such an enigma," Lady Griswall continued, more to herself than to her companion. "He appears in town as if from nowhere, causing quite a stir I might add. Then he remains holed up in his hotel suite for the duration of his stay, eschewing all invitations, some from the premier hostesses of the *ton*."

The premier hostesses? Charlotte was more confused than ever. "Ma'am, who is Mr.—"

"Scarce a fortnight later," her ladyship continued as if Charlotte had not spoken, "the fellow disappears just as mysteriously as he appeared. Without so much as a word of explanation to any of the hostesses who had been so kind as to send him cards of invitation. Quite rag-mannered behavior, you will admit, even for one only just returned from India."

Charlotte was prepared to admit that "rag-mannered," did not come close to describing his actions where *she* was concerned. Unfortunately, her ladyship never gave her the opportunity to finish a sentence. "If you please, ma'am, who—"

"Now, here the fellow is on this walking tour, an

excursion for which he was totally unprepared, if his clothing is anything to judge by. Furthermore, after snubbing a dozen or so of the *bon ton*, he appears to be going out of his way to make himself agreeable to what can only be called a very, er, diversified group of individuals. Curious behavior, I must say. Most curious."

Enigma. Mysterious. Curious. Those were not words to instill serenity in an already disquieted breast, and as Charlotte watched Harrison Montgomery approach Peter and engage the lad in conversation, she, too, wondered what the man was up to.

"A most interesting person," her ladyship muttered beneath her breath. "Hmm. With three rather young gentlemen on the tour, I wonder if . . ." As though suddenly realizing she may have said too much, she paused, then added rather enigmatically, "One would not suppose Mr. Montgomery to be desirous of displaying his skill at skipping stones, would one?"

One would not!

While Charlotte watched the tall gentleman laugh at something Peter had said, some instinct told her that his seeking the lad's company had nothing whatever to do with skipping stones. Though what it did have to do with, she could not even guess.

Who was Mr. Harrison Montgomery, and what had Lady Griswall been about to say? Whatever it might be, Charlotte knew one thing for certain—the man would bear watching.

Chapter Four

"No, sir," Peter answered politely, "neither Jonathan nor I could ever best Charlotte at anything. Running, riding, shooting, even skipping stones, she always won. And do not ask me about swimming, which you will agree is a thing very few females can even do, for she is like some dashed fish."

"Takes to the water, does she?" Harrison said, more interested in studying the lad's face for familiar features than hearing anything he had to say about Miss Charlotte Pelham and her unladylike exploits.

"Like most boys," the youngster continued, "I could not wait to grow up. I, however, had the added incentive of wanting to be taller and stronger than Charlotte so I could defeat her at last."

Harrison looked him over from head to toe. Though the lad was a long way from manhood, without the first sign of a whisker on his smooth face, there could be little doubt that he had at last outgrown Miss Pelham. "And have you put your newfound growth and strength to the test?"

The boy sighed as if much put-upon. "How can I? Now that my dreams are come true, I begin to suspect that it would be ungentlemanly of me to pit my skills against any female's, even Charlotte's."

"Most ungentlemanly," Harrison agreed. Hoping

to trip up the lad, he said, "Have you known her long?"

"Cannot ever remember not knowing her." Having said this, he immediately turned his face away so all Harrison saw was the back of his head. And yet, Harrison would swear he noticed a bit of color stain the lad's cheek.

Harrison's mother had always blushed when called upon to speak anything but the complete truth. Was this young man the same? Was he, in fact, Ann Montgomery James's youngest son? Could he be Timmy? Perhaps, but Harrison would need more proof than a fairly universal tendency to blush.

Like his mother, Harrison possessed gray eyes and medium brown hair, but from the first Timmy had resembled the detested Thomas James, with his dark brown hair and brown eyes. Of course, the lad called Jonathan had similar coloring, as did Miss Pelham. Damnation! Either of the boys could be her brother!

Knowing there was only one way to get the answers he needed, Harrison persevered. "You and Mr. Jonathan Pelham are much the same height and size. So much so that it is difficult to judge which of you is the older. I suspect many people believe you and he to be twins?"

"Very true," Peter replied, offering nothing further on the subject.

"But you are not?"

The lad shook his head. As if to put an end to the inquisition, he skipped one final stone across the water, then brushed his palms together to remove any lingering dirt. "If you will excuse me, sir, I believe my sister has need of me."

Because Miss Charlotte Pelham was, indeed, signaling to the lad to come to her, Harrison took this momentary defeat in good part. This was only the first day, and with a fortnight to go, he was certain

he could learn the truth before they reached the end
of the journey. All he had garnered from this first
interview was that the lad calling himself Peter Pelham was either truly Miss Pelham's brother, or else
he had rehearsed his story well.

Not that it mattered. Harrison was convinced he
would have the truth in due time, for during his
years with the East India Company he had dealt with
liars and dissemblers from nearly every country on
the globe. With such experience behind him, getting
the truth from two youths just out of school should
prove easy enough. As for the woman posing as their
sister, she might not be so easily coerced into revealing which boy was her real brother.

Harrison found himself smiling, for thoughts of
Miss Charlotte Pelham had brought to mind her soft,
pearly skin and those dark, gypsy eyes. With such
enticements, coercing the hoyden could prove more
enjoyable than he had at first supposed. Like the
boys, he might enjoy pitting his more mature skills
against hers.

"Easy, there, old girl," Peter said. "Someone will
hear you."

Taking the correction without rancor, Charlotte
lowered her voice. "What did he want?"

Peter shrugged his shoulders. "A nice chap, actually. I should imagine he was just being friendly."

Charlotte did not believe that for a minute. Like
Lady Griswall, she suspected Harrison Montgomery
was up to something. "What did he say?"

"Nothing much. At least nothing more than I have
heard anytime these past dozen years. He merely remarked that Jonathan and I could pass for twins."

"Peter! Please tell me you did not say anything to
give us away."

He drew himself up to his full height. "Of course I did not. Honestly, Charlie, you treat Jonathan and me like we were still in leading strings. We made you a promise, and a gentleman always honors his word."

Gentleman. If the matter had not been so serious, Charlotte would have laughed aloud. Since when did those two scapegraces become gentlemen? "Your pardon," she said, half jokingly. "I did not mean to impugn your integrity."

"Apology accepted," Peter said, making her a very grown-up bow. "And now," he added, spoiling the effect, "when do we eat? On my oath, old girl, I could eat a pair of oxen. Yoke, nose rings, and all."

As if by common consent, each of the ramblers found shaded spots on the greensward and began emptying their respective haversacks, discovering what the inn chef had packed for their first alfresco meal.

The collations consisted of thinly shaved ham wedged between thick slices of crusty bread, paper twists filled with succession-house raspberries, and flasks of tea; the ladies also supplied shallow bowls from which to drink their tea. No one found fault with the simple repast—their appetites being sharpened by the morning's exercise—and they ate with varying degrees of gusto, leaving not a crumb for the pair of hopeful red squirrels who chattered from the limbs of a nearby birch tree.

Following the meal, the senior Mr. Vinton made his way to where Charlotte and Peter sat, engaging them in conversation that began with a query as to how many times they had made similar long-distance walks.

"I have been on dozens of rambles," Charlotte replied. "My father was an ardent outdoorsman and climber, and he and I went wherever time and weather permitted. Often with no set destination in mind."

"And were you ever lost, ma'am?" the younger Mr. Vinton asked, joining his brother.

"Never lost," she replied. "Though the phrase, 'temporarily misplaced' applied more than once."

The gentlemen laughed, inspiring more of the party to join the group.

"A good compass never comes amiss," Mr. Thorne replied shyly, reaching inside his coat and extracting a small leather pouch. "May I show you my compass, Miss Pelham?"

Harrison had not failed to notice the ever-growing number of gentlemen gathered around Miss Pelham, nor had he been unaware of their obvious enjoyment of her company. Whatever they were discussing, it had occasioned laughter more than once. Had he been allowed to enjoy his meal in private, Harrison would have already packed his haversack and strolled the fifteen yards or so that separated him from Miss Pelham's group.

Regrettably, Colonel Fitzgibbon had seen fit to invite himself to share Harrison's bit of private shade, and the military man had kept up an unceasing flow of chatter. ". . . is worth two in the bush, eh what?" the colonel offered, while Harrison strove in vain to hear what was being discussed fifteen yards away.

Politeness could carry the day only so far, and Harrison was wondering if anyone would notice if he murdered the colonel and left his body beneath the tree, when he saw Lady Griswall finish the last of her tea and return the shallow bowl to her haversack. Excusing himself to the colonel on the pretext of helping her ladyship to stand, he hurried over to her. "Lady Griswall," he said, offering her his hand, "allow me."

"Why, thank you, Mr. Montgomery."

Once the lady was on her feet, she looked from Harrison to the little group gathered around Miss Pelham and her brother, then pushed her tongue purposefully into her cheek. "I would have thought, sir, that you would have hurried over to offer your assistance to Miss Pelham, she being surrounded by all the *young* gentlemen."

Silently Harrison cursed that damned advertisement he had been so foolish as to put in the London papers. First it had brought him all manner of imposters hoping to convince him that they were his long-lost brother, and now it seemed it was about to trip him up again. "Lady Griswall," he said, turning upon her all the charm at his disposal, "pray pardon my curiosity, but did you by chance read a certain advertisement that appeared in the London papers?"

"Even if I had not read it for myself, sir, the entire *ton* spoke of little else. My own sister-in-law, Lady Barrett, must have concocted at least a dozen schemes for putting her daughter in your way. She and every other matchmaking mama in town formed a regular parade, strolling up and down Piccadilly day after day and pausing for long stretches of time in front of Pulteney's Hotel, their hope to accidentally meet the mysterious nabob who was reputed to have amassed a rather sizeable fortune. What possessed you, sir, to make the thing public? Too foolish by half."

"Where were you, ma'am, when I needed a wiser head?"

Her ladyship chuckled. "Sitting in my brother-in-law's town house in Grosvenor Square, marking off the days until I could make my escape."

Harrison smiled. "I see we are kindred spirits, ma'am, for I, too, could not wait to be away."

"Yes, but I am persuaded that my leaving did not set the town on its ear, as yours must have done."

Deeming the time right, Harrison ventured to change the subject. "I wonder, ma'am, if I might prevail upon you for a favor."

Lady Griswall was no more immune than the next woman to the blandishments of a handsome, roguish gentleman, especially one whose past was probably little better than that of a pirate. "A favor, sir? Pray, what sort of favor?"

"Nothing too complicated, ma'am. I just wondered if you would be so good as to allow that advertisement to be our little secret. You see, it brought all manner of scoundrels to my hotel, and I had hoped to avoid them for a time by going on this little outing."

The lady gave him a measuring look. "So, you wished to put the matter aside for a time, did you?"

"I knew you would understand."

"But I do not understand, sir. Not half an hour ago, when I saw you down by the water's edge, I formed an entirely different opinion of your reason for being here. It looked to me, sir, as if you were, shall we say, getting better acquainted with a young person who is of similar age to the brother mentioned in the advertisement."

"Pure coincidence, ma'am." He lifted the hand he still held in his and pressed a kiss on the lady's knuckles. "May I depend upon your discretion, ma'am?"

She sighed as if much put-upon, but the indulgent smile upon her lips told its own story. "It would be a shame," she said, "if any of those scoundrels you mentioned should appear and spoil this lovely walk."

"Madam, you are most kind."

"However," she cautioned, "you must know that your quest was the subject of numerous conversations among the *ton*, and should anything of an 'in-

teresting' nature occur during this cross-country
journey, I expect to be the first to know. If I should
be the one to deliver the news to the *ton*, my sister-
in-law would be pea green with envy."

"Madam," he said, making her a deep, courtly
bow, "pea green is my favorite color."

Having arrived at an understanding with the only
person likely to give him away, Harrison excused
himself and strolled over to the group gathered around
Miss Pelham, more curious than he wanted to admit
as to what she was saying to draw all the young men
to her side.

"But I must disagree," the younger Mr. Vinton
said, as if continuing with a discussion already in
progress, "for without a compass, Miss Pelham, or at
least some familiar landmark, a person might easily
become lost."

"Not," Mr. Andrew Vinton added politely, "that
Lawrence doubts your word, ma'am."

"No, ma'am!" the younger gentleman declared vehemently, his face a study in shades of red. "Meant
nothing of the sort, I assure you. It is just that . . .
that—"

"It is just," the solicitor continued, "that Lawrence
and I are rather new to cross-country walking, and
we wondered what we should do if by some mis-
judgment we became separated from the group."

"I would like to know as well," Wilfred Bryce said,
"if you'll pardon my asking."

Peter moved to stand at Charlotte's side in a famil-
ial gesture that did not go unnoticed by Harrison.
"Show them, Charlie," the lad said. As if certain of
her acquiescence, he dumped the tea leaves from her
bowl and said he would get the water. "You find a
suitable leaf."

While Peter went to the lake's edge and filled the
shallow bowl to the brim, Miss Pelham looked about

her for a leaf. When the proper foliage was found—
one small enough to fit easily inside the bowl—she
dug into her haversack and withdrew a card of pins.

Within a matter of minutes, the entire party was
gathered around her. "First," she said, taking the
bowl of water from Peter, "you must place the recep-
tacle on a flat surface, so the leaf can remain level."
Suiting the action to the word, she placed the bowl
on the ground; then, she placed the leaf on top of
the water, allowing it to float.

"This is all very interesting, I'm sure," Wilfred
Bryce said, "but I fail to see how a leaf in water can
possibly—"

"A moment, if you please," Miss Pelham replied.

Harrison had a pretty good idea what came next,
but he remained silent, not wishing to spoil the show.

While he watched, Miss Pelham took one of the
pins and rubbed it rather vigorously against the
sleeve of her habit for several seconds. "And now,"
she said, her dark eyes sparkling with enjoyment,
"one has only to lay the pin very carefully in the
center of the leaf, and *voila*! There is compass enough
for any traveler."

As the crowd leaned forward to look inside the
bowl, the leaf turned slowly, as if by magic, until the
pin resting on it pointed due north. Mr. Russell
Thorne removed his own compass and laid it beside
the bowl. Both needles pointed in the same direction.

"By Jove," the colonel uttered.

Lady Griswall applauded. "Brava, Miss Pelham."

"Here, here," both the Vinton brothers added.

"How clever," Dora Richardson said. "Does it
work every time?"

"Every time," Peter assured her.

"Most interesting," Wilfred Bryce declared, but if
his praise lacked sincerity, only Harrison seemed to
notice. Not that it mattered overmuch, for as soon as

the demonstration was finished, each of the ramblers repacked his or her haversack in readiness for the second and final part of the day's journey.

"Ambleside, here we come," Peter said, his boyish enthusiasm drawing the younger Mr. Vinton to his side. As the two young gentlemen strode away from the lake, to return to the path, Harrison fell in beside Miss Pelham.

"An excellent job with the compass, ma'am. Have you more tricks concealed inside your sleeve?"

"One or two," she replied, her tone not at all inviting. "And what of you, Mr. Montgomery? What have you got up your sleeve?"

He pretended to misunderstand her. "I? I am not given to tricks, ma'am."

"No?" The look she gave him said all too plainly that she did not believe him. "How very odd, for my instincts are usually quite reliable, and at the moment those instincts tell me that you are concealing something."

He put his hand over his heart, as if wounded. "Madam, do I detect a note of suspicion?"

"A note? Mr. Montgomery, my suspicions of you constitute an entire symphony."

A good half hour later, the memory of Harrison Montgomery's laughter still rang in Charlotte's ears. Drat the man! Did he have no shame? Apparently not. Not if he could blackmail her one day, then try to turn her up sweet the next. Excellent job, indeed! She wanted none of his compliments.

She had turned and walked away, and thank goodness he had not attempted to catch up with her. She had said all she meant to say to him for a time; besides, she had other things on her mind. Far more serious things than solving the mystery of Mr. Harrison Montgomery. The group would be in Ambleside within a matter of hours, and once they reached the Ghyll Inn, where "Charles" was supposed to be waiting for them, Charlotte would be obliged to confess her deception.

The ramblers had appeared satisfied with the morning's walk and had found pleasure in the small lake where they stopped for their meal. Furthermore, they had shown a flattering interest in her compass demonstration, treating her and her knowledge with respect. Unfortunately, people were notoriously changeable, and when she was finally obliged to inform them that there was no Mr. Charles Pelham and that it was *she* who was to be their leader, they might turn on her in an instant.

Not that she could do anything about it if they did; nothing except promise to have every last farthing of their tour money returned to them. The London travel agency would reimburse them for all the uncompleted portion of the tour, but it suddenly occurred to Charlotte that it would be up to her to pay for that first night's lodging.

Suddenly her lips felt drier than day-old toast. She had no funds of her own, and if she were obliged to reimburse everyone for the night spent at the White Rose Inn, at St. Bee's Head, she would have to borrow the money from her mother's new husband. That worthy, though not as rigid as some clergymen, had been astonished at the idea of Charlotte pursuing such an unladylike occupation, and if she failed, and he was obliged to pay the piper for his new stepdaughter, his dismay might well turn to dislike.

At the time Charlotte had been negotiating with the London travel agency, they had informed her that another person had applied for the job as tour guide—a man with good credentials. As it happened, the other applicant had less experience than Mr.

Charles Pelham on that particular walk, so the agency had given the assignment to Charles.

For all Charlotte knew, that other applicant was still waiting in London, hoping "Mr. Pelham" would fail, so he could take over as guide for the next cross-country walking tour. What, she wondered, would that unknown man think if he knew there was no Charles Pelham? How would he react? Would he be angry? Would the travel agency be angry?

Even if every last rambler agreed to continue with Charlotte as guide, and everything on the tour went smoothly, there was still a chance the travel agency would refuse to keep her in their employ. In that event, all future tours would be given to that other guide, and Charlotte would be obliged to seek more "feminine" employment. She shuddered, not wanting even to contemplate such a depressing future.

All too aware that she might well have only a few more hours as leader of this amiable group, Charlotte determined to enjoy the next few hours. After all, whatever would happen at Ambleside would happen; worrying at this late date would change nothing.

Resolved to let the future take care of itself, she adjusted the knapsack on her back and gave herself up to the pleasant song of a wagtail.

"A delightful bird, the pied wagtail."

Charlotte had thought she was alone, but she managed to smile at Mr. Russell Thorne, who walked so softly she had not even known he was close by.

"The little fellow is perched just there," he said, pointing to a trio of sheep who had strayed from the flock that grazed a good quarter of a mile away. The dainty bird, with its white breast and its coal-colored back, was perched on one of the sheep's horns, obviously treating himself to some bug that had chanced to light there first.

"I love all the feathered creatures," Mr. Thorne

said, "but none are so dear to my heart as the wagtail."

Not certain how to reply, Charlotte said, "A very English bird, to be sure."

For the next half hour, the gentleman treated Charlotte to a most interesting lesson in ornithology. He had introduced himself yesterday as a climber and a birder, but after thirty minutes in his company she decided his shyness had prompted him toward modesty. His knowledge of bird life proclaimed him an expert on the subject as surely as his compact, yet muscular physique gave evidence of his climbing experience and probable expertise.

Here was a gentleman who would make an excellent tour guide. Charlotte could only hope that if she was so unfortunate as to lose her job with the travel agency, her replacement would be as competent as Mr. Russell Thorne.

Chapter Five

Though the afternoon's walk had been enjoyable, Charlotte readily admitted to herself that she would be happy to reach the Ghyll Inn, situated just outside Ambleside. During the past two hours, the path had begun to rise steadily, making the walking much more taxing, so much so that when they passed a bobbin mill scarcely a quarter of an hour from Ambleside, the group voted unanimously to make a brief stop.

During the respite, everyone took a turn looking at the distant fells through Mr. Thorne's Claude glass. A peculiar sort of instrument, the glass, when closed, fit into a case that resembled a small book. When in use, the upper part of the instrument was extended above the holder's head; then the viewer turned his back on the object he wished to view, thereby shielding his face from the sun.

While the others walked around to the rear of the factory to have a drink from the well, Charlotte took a turn viewing the scenery through the glass. Though the fells were at this point more hills than mountains, they were still beautiful, with distant waters appearing like thin ribbons of silver that gently threaded their way along the rocky hillsides.

The land surrounding the bobbin mill was alive with color, forming a carpet of fresh green foliage sprinkled here and there with white wood anemones and full-faced dandelions. Nearby, softly bleating sheep grazed unhurriedly, while the late-afternoon sun shone through a tracery of spring buds bursting on the trees.

"A penny for your thoughts," Mr. Harrison Montgomery said quietly, very close to Charlotte's ear. "What think you of the Claude glass?"

"Only a penny?" she asked, closing the instrument and shutting the case with a definite snap. "I collect you mean to make sport of me, sir—me being country bred, and without your jaded palate and your vast knowledge of the world—so I protest that a penny is rather a miserly price for your entertainment."

A teasing light appeared in his gray eyes. "Make sport of you? Upon my oath, ma'am, nothing was further from my mind."

Placing no faith in his vow, she did not give her opinions into his keeping. Instead, she said, "Did you not hear the others? To a man, they marveled at the way the glass made the scenery appear as though it were an illustration in a book."

"An example, I am persuaded, of that fable about some emperor and his new clothes."

Secretly, Charlotte was of the same opinion; however, she countered by tilting her head and looking directly into Mr. Montgomery's eyes, declaring herself positively agog to know what *he* thought. "Did you not find the view through the glass wonderful?"

He did not answer right away. Instead, he gave her look for look, holding her gaze so long and so intently that she became uncomfortable and wished she might avert her eyes. Unfortunately, she had never looked away first in her life, and she would not do so now.

Charlotte held her own in the visual battle, though the seconds dragged like hours. When she thought she might scream from the strain of not blinking, the infuriating man chuckled and let his gaze move slowly down to her mouth, an action that relieved one discomfort while producing another.

"No fair," he said softly, his gaze lingering on her mouth, "I offered you a penny for your thoughts, yet you sought mine without proposing so much as a farthing in remuneration. Had you other payment in mind?"

Other payment? Surely he did not mean what she thought he meant. Or did he?

To Charlotte's dismay, he leaned toward her slightly, as if he intended to kiss her. She remained completely still—she could not have moved if her life had depended upon it—and as if she had lost complete control of her body, she felt her lips pucker.

She thought she heard his indrawn breath, but before she could be certain, he straightened as though he had never meant to do more than shift his weight. Completely ignoring her expectant lips, he continued as if nothing had happened. "As in most things, Miss Pelham, I and my jaded palate prefer the view as nature made it, without benefit of artifice. What of you?"

Try as she might, Charlotte could not answer his question, for the words would not come. Moments earlier, she had felt a pleasant fluttering in her midsection in anticipation of her first kiss. A kiss that had obviously existed only in her mind. Now, mortification at her own foolish reaction had turned that fluttering into a tight knot that moved from its original position to lodge in her throat.

Heat engulfed her. What on earth had made her think that Harrison Montgomery, of all people, was about to kiss her?

And why, in heaven's name, had she puckered?

"Miss Pelham," the younger Mr. Vinton said,

breaking in upon her embarrassing thoughts, "may I have the Claude glass? If you are quite finished, that is."

More grateful than she could say for the interruption, she gave Lawrence Vinton the case. "I . . . I am quite finished," she said. "Forgive me, for I had not meant to monopolize it." When he took the glass and turned to walk away, she went with him, not giving Mr. Montgomery so much as a backward glance.

When they resumed their walk, Charlotte told Peter to take the lead again, while she dropped back to bring up the rear. The solitude gave her some much-needed time in which to regain her composure after making a fool of herself, and while she followed the group, she noticed that Mr. Richardson was lagging behind slightly, and that Colonel Fitzgibbon had wisely stanched his flow of platitudes and was conserving his breath.

With such obvious signs of fatigue among the group, Charlotte was glad they had only a quarter of a mile more to travel. She was delighted when they crossed a footbridge whose pinkish stone spanned a gently gurgling beck, for it meant their destination was but a few minutes away. Having traveled this route more than once, she knew that the gurgling of the beck would soon give way to the far more dramatic sound of a force, or waterfall, where the Ambleside ghyll flowed over a stretch of sun-bleached boulders and plunged its way down to the gorge below.

Just beyond the force stood the inn. Or perhaps "perched" was a better word.

Her first sight of Ghyll Inn always made Charlotte's breath catch in her throat, for the lovely old limestone building appeared to be balanced on the very edge of the gorge. At the moment, the westering sun had streaked the sky in cobalt blue and bright orange, and the dramatic colors merely added to the inn's otherworldly look.

As she expected, hers was not the only gasp of approval. "Oh, my," Lady Griswall muttered. "Words fail me."

"One picture," the colonel informed her, "is worth a thousand words."

Thankfully, her ladyship chose not to take offense, and the ramblers, their weariness all but forgotten, moved cautiously toward the rim of the steep-sided gorge. For several moments, they observed in silence the panoramic view; then they began to call to one another's attention the tiny cottages that clung as if by magic to the lower slopes.

"An opportune moment," Mr. Montgomery said, surprising her yet again with the quietness with which he moved, "to make your confession about Mr. Charles Pelham. Now, while everyone is speechless with awe."

Charlotte did not bother pretending to misunderstand him, and though he was the last person in the world she wanted to speak to, she thanked him for his advice, her tone just cool enough to let him know that she was not the least bit appreciative. "However," she added, "I believe I would do better to wait until I have everyone's attention."

"I cannot agree. As Colonel Fitzgibbon would say, 'timing is everything.' In such a setting as this, your disclosure that you have, shall we say, manufactured brothers as the need arose, might well fade into insignificance."

Since Mr. Montgomery continued to offer his wholly unsolicited advice, and he would not take the hint to go away and to stop tormenting her, Charlotte resorted to bluntness. "Forgive me for stating the obvious, sir, but there is not the least reason for you to concern yourself about this business. The matter of my brothers—real or invented—is none of your affair, so I beg you will trouble yourself with them no longer."

"But I assure you," he said, paying no more attention to bluntness than he did to subtle hints, "it is no trouble at all."

Drat the man! Must she beat him with a stick to get her point across?

"As for myself," he continued pleasantly, "you need have no fear. I have no intention of leaving this tour, no matter who leads it."

"Considering the fact that you blackmailed your way into the group, I am not surprised that you mean to remain. I just wish I knew why."

"Must one have a reason?"

She shook her head. "A *reason* is not required, but somehow I cannot rid myself of the belief that there is a *motive* behind your unexpected arrival and your dogged determination to stay."

With that, she turned and walked away, and if she felt Harrison watching her, she gave no indication of it.

And he did watch. Though her steps were purposeful, there was a decidedly feminine sway to her rounded hips, a sway that reminded him that he was a man who had been without female companionship for more weeks than he cared to remember. Not that Charlotte Pelham was anything like the voluptuous barques of frailty he usually chose to entertain— women whose one objective was to please their man.

Which was not to say that Charlotte Pelham would be incapable of pleasing a man. Far from it. The more Harrison got to know her, the more he was obliged to revise his first impression of her. True, she was athletic. And true again, she had no business being here, attempting to do a man's job, but he had been mistaken in summarily dismissing her as one of those pathetic females who wished to be a man.

She was outspoken, determined, and confident in her own abilities—perhaps overly confident—but nothing in her deportment or her appearance was in the least mannish. Furthermore, any male with blood in his veins could be forgiven for wanting to run his fingers through her lustrous black hair or touch that flawless skin. As for her mouth—

Harrison gave himself a mental shake. He was acting like a moonling, or one of those insufferable young puppies who wrote insipid odes to some female's eyebrow!

But then, it was not Charlotte Pelham's eyebrow that was making him irritable. It was the memory of those pink lips that had puckered so invitingly earlier.

He could not remember what had given him the completely wild notion of kissing her, but he had leaned toward her with no other thought in his mind than tasting her lips, forgetting that he and the object of his attention were within sight of any number of observers. And he would have kissed her, too, had she not puckered like a very young, very innocent girl awaiting her first kiss.

A first kiss needed to be sweet and meaningful, even if the female was no longer a girl. And if it was her first, which appeared more than likely, even the headstrong Miss Pelham deserved something better than a spur-of-the-moment buss before an audience.

Harrison was still thinking of that aborted kiss when he was suddenly snatched back to the moment by a hair-raising scream that came from the direction of the gorge. It was a woman's scream—a scream soon followed by all manner of masculine yells and curses.

"Dora!" young Mr. Richardson yelled.

"Help him!" Lady Griswall called to no one in particular.

The "him" in question was Wilfred Bryce, who was on his knees in the dusty red soil, holding with all his might to something that had gone over the rim of the gorge.

As Harrison ran to help, he saw the colonel, with the aid of Mr. Thorne, forcibly detaining Mr. Richardson, while Peter and Mr. Andrew Vinton fell to their stomachs and reached over to assist Bryce in retrieving whatever had fallen over the side. Only when he arrived at the rim did Harrison realize that the "something" was Dora Richardson.

Bryce relinquished his place to Vinton and moved away from the edge; then, totally spent, he stretched out on the ground, his breathing understandably ragged and his right arm cradled against his side. Knowing that too many helpers often caused more problems than they solved, Harrison did not go all the way to the edge. Instead, he caught Peter and Vinton by their ankles to help steady them as they strained to pull the young woman back from the threat of certain death. Once the near-victim's blond head and blue-clad shoulders were clearly visible, and the time was right for intervention, Harrison reached over Peter and caught the young lady beneath her arms, pulling her toward him, her feet dragging across the exhausted young man's back.

Though she was ashen faced, she fought valiantly to resist fainting, and the moment her feet touched solid ground, Harrison lifted her in his arms and carried her to where her husband was being held. Mr. Richardson's legs had given way beneath him, and if the colonel and Thorne had not supported him, he would have fallen to the ground. Because the young fellow looked every bit as close to fainting as did his bride, Harrison continued to hold her securely in his arms, allowing Mr. Richardson to put his face against his wife's, their tears mingling in combined fear and relief.

"Bring her into the inn," Charlotte Pelham said, appearing as if from nowhere. "Lady Griswall's maid has run ahead to the Richardsons' room to light a fire and turn back the covers on the bed, and I have sent one of the ostlers to the village to fetch the physician."

Always more than happy to acquiesce to sensible instruction, Harrison followed Charlotte into the inn and up a flight of narrow stairs, with Mr. Richardson and his two helpers close behind. Only when he had laid the still-weeping young lady on the bed did Harrison step back and allow Miss Pelham to take over. "What do you need?" he asked.

"Room," she replied in her no-nonsense manner. "The landlord is sending up a pitcher of hot water so I can clean the lady's wounds. Meanwhile, I believe Mr. Richardson would be better for a glass of brandy."

"I am not leaving her!" the young man cried out.

"Of course not," Harrison said, putting his hand on the young fellow's shoulder and gently compelling him to sit in the room's only chair. "You will stay here to offer your wife the support of your presence. And while Miss Pelham administers to her, I will send the crowd away and see that a glass of brandy is brought up immediately."

He turned back to Charlotte, who knelt on the faded Turkey carpet beside the bed, cooing reassurances to the trembling girl while she unfastened the snug habit so the young lady could breathe more easily. "I will be at the bottom of the stairs, Miss Pelham. Should you need anything—anything at all—you have only to call out. I will hear you."

She glanced his way for an instant, nodded, then returned her attention to Dora Richardson.

Twilight had come and gone before Charlotte saw Mr. Montgomery again. He had been most helpful during the hour following the accident, relaying Charlotte's needs to the appropriate servant and seeing that his orders were carried out.

After the physician had declared the patient free of injury save for a dislocated shoulder, he had given her a dose of laudanum, then departed. Minutes later, Mr. Montgomery had knocked at the bedchamber door and handed Charlotte a small tray containing a cup of hot, fragrant tea and a bowl of thick broth. "Eat every drop," he said, motioning toward the still-steaming broth.

With the enormity of what might have happened preying on her mind, Charlotte was anything but hungry, but she did as he instructed, knowing full well that she would need her strength for later. Her ordeal was not over, for she had still to get through the confession to the group about her spurious brother, Charles.

When she finally left the patient in the capable hands of one of the kitchen maids, Charlotte went to her own room to freshen up before going below stairs to face the rest of the group. At Peter's request, they had all assembled in the private parlor set aside for their meals—all save Wilfred Bryce, who had been helped to his room, considerably jug bitten.

Bryce had figured as the hero in the near tragedy, having been the one to grab Mrs. Richardson's wrist as she slipped over the rim, then held on to her using only one arm until the others arrived. As a consequence, every male in the taproom—gentlemen and locals alike—had insisted on standing him to a tankard of ale. Needless to say, no one begrudged him his present state of inebriation, least of all Charlotte. In fact, had she been available earlier, she would have insisted on purchasing a round as well to show her gratitude.

As the leader of the group, she felt responsible for everyone's safety, even though logic told her that she could not have foreseen the near fatality. In truth, how could anyone have foreseen such a mystifying turn of events?

The young bride had seemed far too sensible to get that close to the edge of the gorge. Furthermore, she was as graceful as she could stare. That Dora Richardson should lose her footing was perplexing enough, but that her knight in shining armor should prove to be Wilfred Bryce—the clumsiest man it had ever been Charlotte's misfortune to meet—was nothing short of mind-boggling.

Chapter Six

"Let me begin," Charlotte said, her voice not as steady as she could have wished, "by thanking all of you for your assistance this afternoon. But for your quick thinking, a young woman would now be lying at the bottom of the gorge. Thankfully, aside from the understandable fright, Mrs. Richardson has suffered no more than a dislocated shoulder and a few scrapes and bruises. She and her husband have both asked me to express their appreciation to each and every one of you. They consider you all heroes of the first order."

Murmured protestations filled the small private parlor, as those seated around the oak table denied that their actions were anything out of the ordinary. When there was silence once again, Charlotte continued. "Needless to say, the Richardsons will not be continuing with us. They both agreed that it would be best if, after a few days' rest, they returned to their home by post."

"Always a treat," Colonel Fitzgibbon said, "to discover wise heads on young bodies."

For once, no one appeared to find fault with his cliché.

"We shall miss them," her ladyship said.

"Quite," the colonel agreed.

"Miss Pelham," Mr. Andrew Vinton said, "please forgive what may sound a most insensitive question, but how will this accident affect the tour? Will we continue tomorrow as planned, or must—that is to say, *will*—we remain here until Mrs. Richardson is well enough to travel?"

"I, too, have a question," Mr. Thorne said, "and I hope, ma'am, that it will not add to your concerns."

"What is that, sir?"

"Though I have looked about the grounds, and even asked after him, no one seems to have any knowledge as to the whereabouts of your brother, Mr. Charles Pelham. Mrs. Richardson's injuries notwithstanding, how are we to continue the tour without our guide?"

The moment had come, and now that it was here, Charlotte's knees began to tremble. She placed her hands on the edge of the table for support. How, after all that had happened today, was she to own up to a falsehood of such monumental proportions? She would not blame the others if they threatened to draw and quarter her.

As if sensing her trepidation, Peter and Jonathan, who had remained out of the way at the rear of the room, came to stand beside her. Grateful for their loyalty, even though they had both initially proclaimed the scheme completely harebrained, Charlotte drew a deep breath and began. "Lady Griswall. Gentlemen. There is no Mr. Charles Pelham."

Several people spoke at once. "What? Surely you jest, Miss Pelham."

"It is no jest. I have no older brother. I . . . I made him up."

The colonel sprang to his feet. "Made him up!"

Unable to deny it, Charlotte nodded.

"But, ma'am," the younger Mr. Vinton said, "what had you to gain by such a deception?"

"Never mind that," Colonel Fitzgibbon interrupted. "What about the tour? What of the blunt I put down? This is intolerable, young woman. I consider it nothing short of fraud."

Charlotte was obliged to clear her throat to remove the very large frog that had taken up residence there. "On my honor, Colonel, no fraud was intended. I merely invented an older brother so that I might gain employment with the travel agency."

She looked about the group, hoping to find at least one face that did not show contempt. To her relief, Colonel Fitzgibbon was the only person who was openly hostile; the others appeared more perplexed than angry.

"I needed employment, and the moment I read about this proposed new cross-country walking tour, I knew without doubt that I was the perfect person to act as guide. The advertisement did not *say* that only males should apply. All the same, I knew the travel agency would not even consider my application. Not at first. Not without unassailable proof that I could do the job."

"And rightly so, young woman!"

"But in all fairness, Colonel, how was I to present proof without actually leading a tour?"

The military gentleman either could not or would not answer. Instead, he reclaimed his chair, muttering something about females and convoluted logic.

Let the poets insist that confession is good for the soul; at the moment Charlotte felt no such inner cleansing. In fact, her stomach threatened to return the broth she had eaten earlier. Wanting to have this meeting over before that embarrassment was added to her other sins, she took one last deep breath and finished in a rush. "I realize that every one of you may feel you cannot trust my word, not after I began our association with a falsehood, but I *am* fully qualified to lead this tour, having traveled it many times with my father."

"But . . . but," Colonel Fitzgibbon sputtered, "you are a female."

Leave it to him to state the obvious!

Somehow, his remark stiffened Charlotte's spine, and she was able to continue. "Yes, Colonel, I am a female. That is a fact I cannot deny. And though I feel that my ability, and not my sex, should be the primary concern here, I am not so foolish as to believe that others will share that opinion. For that reason, if any of you feel that you cannot continue on this walking tour with a female as your guide, please say so now. Naturally, for those of you who choose not to continue, your money will be refunded."

For a time, no one spoke; then Mr. Montgomery rose and faced the remaining five members of the tour, his height and his muscular form gaining him their attention without any need on his part to ask for it. "My reasons for joining this tour have not changed," he said quietly. "Therefore, I mean to continue."

Lady Griswall had watched Mr. Montgomery, a smile upon her face, almost as if she knew his reasons for staying. Following his lead, she rose, and when she spoke, her response, like his, was positive. "Leave now? Wild horses could not tear me away."

"Nor I," Mr. Thorne said. "There are birds to be observed and mountains to be climbed, and I have looked forward to this trip with too much anticipation to allow some minor misrepresentations to spoil it for me."

"Minor misrepresentations!" The colonel all but choked on the words. "Have you all gone mad? She is a *female*!"

"And what has that to say to anything?" Lady Griswall asked, her frosty tone leaving no doubt as to what she thought of mere colonels who questioned a decision by a member of the nobility. "I, too, am a female."

Obviously not grasping her ladyship's point, the military gentleman said, "But Miss Pelham is a *young* female, while you are an—"

"Speaking for my brother and myself," Mr. Andrew Vinton interjected quickly, "nothing would give us greater pleasure than to continue the tour with Miss Pelham as our guide. Especially if she is willing to share with us some more of her woodland knowledge. That leaf-compass was ingenious."

"Here, here!" the younger Mr. Vinton said.

At the five votes of confidence, Charlotte felt moisture pool in her eyes, and though she willed herself not to blink and dislodge the tears, one lone droplet managed to escape, slipping slowly down her cheek. Mortified, she turned her back to the group and quickly brushed the betraying moisture aside.

"Here now!" the colonel said. "Let us have no tears. In the interest of esprit de corps, I might be persuaded to overlook your other shortcomings, Miss Pelham, but I positively refuse to spend the next fortnight with a cursed watering pot!"

It had come as a disappointment to Harrison and Benizur that the turban-wearing eavesdropper had discovered nothing important about Jonathan.

"The young sahib keeps his own counsel," Benizur said, placing another shovel of coal into the small stove in the bedchamber. "But I will try again. Perhaps the other one will have more to say."

"I sincerely hope he may. When I tried to engage him in conversation, I discovered only that he can skip rocks across the water and that he is pluck to the backbone."

Harrison smiled, recalling Peter's quickness in rushing to help save Mrs. Richardson. The lad might or might not be *his* brother, but he was undoubtedly a brother to be proud of.

"In any case, my friend, before you do any more investigating, there is another errand to be executed."

"Yes, Sahib?"

"When you reach the next village—Windermere, I believe it is called—I wish you to search out a more suitable jacket for me. It need not be fashionable, nor even new. I require only that it be reasonably clean and appropriate to the more rigorous walks coming up in the next few days. Take one of my coats to judge the size, only get the jacket a bit larger. If I am to climb, I will need more room in the shoulders and back. And," he added, lowering his voice on the odd chance that he might be heard through the walls, "find me a holstered knife."

Benizur bowed slightly. "I will do as you wish, of course, Sahib, but first I should like to know why you feel the need for a weapon. Are you in danger?"

Harrison did not attempt to dissemble, for he had never been able to put anything over on Benizur for very long. "It is the accident. Something about what happened has me puzzled. I am not altogether certain why I have this feeling, but I am convinced that Miss Pelham is not the only person on this tour who has been less than truthful. For now, though, I know only that I feel the need to be watchful. And armed."

A very canny fellow, Benizur asked no more questions. "I, too, will be watchful. After," he added, "I have found Sahib a suitable jacket."

The need for sturdier footwear had been met late Monday evening when a knock on Harrison's bed-chamber door had revealed the inn's bootboy with a letter in one hand and pair of freshly polished walking boots in the other. The letter was from Stephen Richardson.

Dear Mr. Montgomery,

Words cannot express my most sincere appreciation for the part you played in my wife's rescue.

There is no way I can ever hope to repay this debt, but if there is ever a time when I can be of service to you, I beg you will not deny me that opportunity.

In the meantime, please accept these boots. Though I have nothing like your excellent physique, I believe you and I are of a similar height. For that reason, I pray my walking boots will fit you.

In all things I remain,
Yr. Ob. Serv.
Stephen Richardson

Much to Harrison's surprise, the boots proved a near-perfect fit. To his further delight, they had been walked in just enough to make the leather resilient, without molding themselves to the previous wearer's feet.

He gave the bootboy a shilling and asked him to relay his appreciation to Mr. Richardson. "Tell the gentleman that I will give myself the pleasure of stopping by his room in the morning, before the group leaves, to see how Mrs. Richardson fares, and to offer him my thanks in person."

"By Jove," the colonel said the next morning. While lifting the pewter lid from the last of the eight covered dishes set out for those of the guests who wished to break their fasts, he had discovered his favorite meat. "Braised ox tongue. Excellent."

None of the party had possessed much of an appetite last evening while they waited for word of Mrs. Richardson's injuries, so like Jonathan, Peter, Mr. Thorne, and the Vinton brothers, who had already taken their places at the oval table, the military gentleman filled his plate this morning. Turning to Harrison, who had only just entered the room, he recommended the coddled eggs. "And do try one of those bramble-berry tarts."

Though Harrison had not been the least surprised to discover neither of the ladies among the assembled company, he ventured to ask young Jonathan if his "sister" meant to allow herself a much-deserved sleep-in this morning.

"Not Charlie," he replied. "M'sister is made of sterner stuff. She bends, but she never breaks."

"Except her fast," the lady herself added from the doorway. "I always break my fast. Especially when I know there are at least fifteen miles between this and my next hot meal."

All the gentlemen stood at Charlotte's entrance, and Mr. Andrew Vinton held out a chair for her and asked if he might be allowed to serve her.

"That is most gallant of you," she said, not approaching the proffered chair, "but it is imperative on a tour such as this that everyone takes care of his or her own needs. Both Lady Griswall and I are experienced ramblers, and we do not expect any of you gentlemen to cater to us. If at any time we should have need of a bit more strength than we possess, we will speak up immediately. Until then, I will ask that you set aside your chivalry and look upon us as nothing more than fellow travelers."

"Very fetching fellow travelers," the solicitor replied, not yet ready to abandon his gallantry. "If I may be allowed to say so, ma'am, that gold habit is most becoming."

Charlotte chuckled, not at all displeased by the compliment. Considering the events of yesterday— the accident and her disclosure that she had deceived them—she was far too happy just to know that the members of the party were speaking to her. "It is my fondest hope, Mr. Vinton, that you like the color of *both* my habits, for you are destined to see a great deal of them in the next thirteen days."

The gentleman chuckled as well. "Miss Pelham, it will be my pleasure."

Harrison chose not to make such a cake of himself as the solicitor had done, but he did surrender his plate to the lady and lifted the first lid so she might view the selections available. "What say you to some eggs, Miss Pelham? And I understand there is braised ox tongue, if you should like it."

The horrified expression on the lady's face told its own story, prompting Harrison to lean close to her, so only she would hear his remark. "As my old nanny used to warn whenever *I* made a hideous face, 'Have a care, or you might freeze that way.' "

"Did you say 'Hideous'?"

"Afraid so, ma'am."

Though she attempted to school her expression, the amusement in those dark eyes gave her away. "What a thoroughly detestable person."

"Actually, Nanny Clark was rather a sweet old girl. A bit of a disciplinarian, mind you, but—"

"The person to whom I referred, sir, was you."

"Tsk, tsk, Miss Pelham. Did you not say only moments ago that we were to put aside our chivalry?"

"Yes, but I did not mean it as an invitation to say every contemptible thing that popped into your head."

"As to that, ma'am, I assure you I do not mean to say *every* contemptible thing."

"You cannot know, Mr. Montgomery, what a comfort that is to me."

Though her voice was steady enough, Harrison thought he detected a smile tugging at the corners of her lips. Unfortunately, he was not to know for sure, for Lady Griswall chose that moment to enter the parlor, and the gentlemen all stood and made their bows. By the time the amenities were gotten through, Miss Pelham had made her selections and returned to the table, taking the chair once again offered her by the solicitor.

Since Jonathan had driven the cumbersome luggage wagon on the first day, Peter took his turn driving the pair of plodding shire horses on the second. As before, her ladyship's maid sat on the seat next to the driver, while a seriously indisposed Wilfred Bryce lay on a blanket in the back of the wagon, holding his head and moaning with every bump and rut in the road.

On this occasion, the Tilbury did not follow behind the creeping conveyance, for Benizur had driven off early Tuesday morning, on an errand for Harrison.

When the ramblers were outside the Ghyll Inn, preparing to begin the morning's walk, Harrison bid them start without him, for it was his intention to pay a farewell visit to the Richardsons. Just before he turned to go back inside, he spoke privately to Miss Pelham, who appeared a little surprised by his announcement to remain at the inn for a time. "I am putting you to the test, ma'am, to see if you meant it when you said you would not wait for me, should I lag behind."

The lady's cheeks turned a bright pink, but she did not rise to the bait. "Just follow the path, sir, and you should have no difficulty in finding us."

"And if I should get lost? Dare I hope that your attitude toward me has softened somewhat, and that you might drop a trail of bread crumbs for me to follow?"

Though her cheeks were still pink, she looked directly into his eyes. "If you should get lost, Mr.

Montgomery, I bid you try the leaf-compass trick. We will be traveling due south."

Of course, Harrison did not get lost. After listening to Mrs. Richardson's surprisingly clear account of all that had happened to her yesterday at the edge of the gorge, he bid the young couple farewell, then set off down the path.

The final destination for the day was Lake Windermere, the most popular spot in the Lake District, and as Harrison hurried to catch up with the ramblers before they stopped for the midday meal, he had no difficulty in understanding the area's popularity. All around him was unsurpassed beauty.

The blue-gray slate beneath his feet was reasonably soft, and because of its softness it was easily eroded, producing a gentle landscape of rounded hills and lush oak forest, with here and there a scattering of silver birch trees. Foremost among the area's attractions, however, especially for a man wearing boots not yet formed to his feet, was the fact that one need not be a mountaineer to cover the distance.

The climb was slow, but not difficult, and before he knew it, Harrison heard Mr. Thorne's voice. The blond gentleman was explaining to Miss Pelham and Lady Griswall, in his quiet, rather diffident manner, the difference between the combative nature of the sparrow hawk and that of the eagle.

"The eagle," he said, "even the golden eagle, whom many call the monarch of the sky, will often drop his prey when attacked by the fearless, and far more pugnacious sparrow hawk. Like a pirate, the sparrow hawk will attack anything that sails past him."

"How fortunate we are," Miss Pelham said, "to be traveling in the company of an expert ornithologist."

"Oh, no, ma'am," the gentleman said. "I am the merest beginner, I assure you."

"Speaking of sailing," her ladyship said, obviously having had enough of bird life for one day, "how long will we remain at Windermere, Miss Pelham. Will there be time enough for a sail across the lake?"

"I am afraid not, ma'am. Nor time for the gentlemen to try their hand at robbing the lake of its trout and pike."

"For me," Mr. Thorne said, "that will be no sacrifice."

Miss Pelham chuckled. "Not so for my brother. He is a passionate fly fisherman."

Harrison, feeling that he had come at the appropriate moment, walked toward them, making his presence known. "And which brother is that, Miss Pelham? Jonathan or Peter?"

"Which? Er . . . both, actually. What one does, the other does. It has always been that way with them. To see one is to see the other."

Lady Griswall gave Harrison a rather knowing look, then remarked offhandedly, "Such nice lads, Miss Pelham. Polite and pretty behaved, both of them. But for the life of me, I cannot tell which of them is older."

The last thing in the world Charlotte wanted was to be caught in another falsehood, so to avoid further tangling the web of lies, she looked about her for something that would allow her to change the subject. As if in answer to a prayer, a fat badger chose that moment to waddle across the path. The sturdy mammal, with its thick black-and-white fur, was not often seen during the daylight hours, and when he spied the humans, he turned and scurried back to the safety of his sett.

Speaking to no one in particular, Charlotte said, "That reminds me. I must warn the group about the unabashed thievery of some of the woodland creatures."

"Quite right," Mr. Thorne said, "for our furry friends hold nothing sacrosanct. I discovered that the hard way."

"The 'hard' way?" Charlotte could not hide her smile, for it was not difficult to guess how the gentleman had learned his lesson. Since he was only slightly taller than she, she did not have far to look up into his face. "Unless I am much mistaken, sir, you are harboring a story I should dearly love to hear."

Mr. Thorne sighed as if much put-upon. "I see how it is, ma'am. You, being wise to the ways of the forest creatures, are desirous of having a laugh at my expense."

"Oh, no, sir, truly. I—"

"So be it," he said, holding up his hand to silence her. "I will not begrudge you the laughter, but understand that at the time I saw little humor in what happened."

"What *did* happen?" her ladyship asked, as ready as Charlotte to hear a good story.

"One rather warm summer day," Mr. Thorne began, "when I was rambling through a wood in Kent, I came upon a pretty little stream. Because the day was unusually warm, and because there was not another soul around for miles, I decided to take a dip."

"A stream," Charlotte said, already beginning to chuckle. "Pray continue, sir."

"My clothes were damp with perspiration, so as I disrobed, I spread each article out on the ground to let the sun dry them. I could not have been gone more than a quarter of an hour, but when I finished my swim and returned for my clothing, I spied a fat little field mouse sitting beside my boots. The creature had one of my stockings in its paws and was busy nibbling at the toe."

"It is the salt," Charlotte said, trying earnestly to curb her laughter. "The animals seem unable to resist it."

Charlotte might have reclaimed her composure had her ladyship and Mr. Montgomery not joined in the laughter; even so, she bit her bottom lip in an effort at control. "What happened next, Mr. Thorne?"

"Surely you can guess, Miss Pelham. When I attempted to shoo the presumptuous creature away, what does he do but run, my stocking clamped securely between his jaws."

Charlotte was now laughing in earnest, as were her two companions. To Lady Griswall's credit, she controlled her amusement long enough to commiserate with the gentleman on his misadventure. "How distressing for you, Mr. Thorne. Were . . . Were you able to reclaim the article?"

"No, ma'am, I was not. I must have chased that thieving rodent for half a mile, but he eventually outran me."

The picture in Charlotte's mind of the reserved Mr. Thorne chasing through the woods in pursuit of a field mouse was too much for her, and she gave full vent to her amusement. It did not help that her ladyship and Mr. Montgomery were laughing as well. "Please," Charlotte begged, "forgive us, Mr. Thorne."

"Laugh if you must," he said, "I daresay I was a figure of fun. In retrospect, I suppose I was fortunate the creature did not steal my inexpressibles."

At any other time, the mention of a gentleman's breeches might have earned him a snub by the ladies. At that particular moment, however, said ladies were trying so hard not to laugh, that imagining Mr. Thorne chasing after his nether garments—naked as the day he was born—merely sent them into further hoops.

Finally, Charlotte raised the sleeve of her habit to

her cheeks to mop the tears. "Your pardon, Mr. Thorne, but I could not resist. The experience with the mouse could not have been anything but distressing for you, and I am persuaded you will think me a heartless creature for laughing at your expense."

"Not at all, ma'am."

"You are to be congratulated on your forbearance, sir."

"If the truth be known, Miss Pelham, I was well recompensed."

Something in the gentleman's tone put an end to Harrison's amusement, and when he studied the fellow's face, it did not seem to him that Mr. Thorne was at all angry with his audience. In fact, he was looking at Miss Pelham with a decidedly moonstruck expression.

As for the lady, she obviously saw nothing amiss. "Recompensed?" she asked.

"Yes, ma'am," Mr. Thorne said quietly, "for it has always been my opinion that there is no finer sight in nature than that of a pretty lady with a smile on her lips."

Chapter Seven

Pretty lady! Deuce take it, Harrison thought. First Mr. Vinton and now Mr. Thorne. Had the men on this tour nothing better to do than flirt with their guide? Not that Thorne was as obvious in his attempts as the solicitor had been that morning. Vinton, being no more than five- or six-and-twenty, had made a positive cake of himself, paying Miss Pelham compliments on what was, in truth, a very ordinary habit. A gentleman of his age probably said the same sort of thing to any passably attractive female.

As for Thorne, who was slightly older than Harrison's twenty-eight years, at least his compliment had the advantage of not sounding polished by overuse. Furthermore, Russell Thorne was a gentleman, with an estate somewhere or other, Harrison forgot just where. The fellow was educated, and judging by the fine quality and expert tailoring of his clothing, he must enjoy a comfortable living.

He would be a good catch for a female in Charlotte Pelham's circumstances—a female who, by her own admission, needed to seek employment. And for all Harrison knew, Russell Thorne was on the lookout for a wife.

Even so, the fellow had a nerve attempting to set up a flirtation with Miss Pelham right there in front of Harrison—and Lady Griswall, of course. It was not as if the young lady was wholly without protection; she had her brother with her, after all. Two brothers, as far as Thorne and Vinton knew.

She was laughing again at something Thorne had said—a circumstance Harrison found irritating in the extreme—and he began to wonder if he ought to give her a little hint about not encouraging the single gentlemen on the tour. Not that it was anything to *him* what she did. Still, he was older and wiser than she, and he had far more experience of the world. Surely it behooved a man of experience to do all within his power to protect a female who was too green to know about roués and rakes.

Charlotte Pelham was an intelligent female; a hint should be enough to put her on her guard. As Colonel Fitzgibbon would say, "A word to the wise is sufficient."

"I should what!" Charlotte could not believe her ears.

"I merely thought, Miss Pelham, that you might not know where to draw the line with such men. You said yourself that you were country bred, and so I—"

"So you took it upon yourself to give me instruction on how a lady should behave."

"You choose to misunderstand me, Miss Pelham. I am not so rag-mannered as to instruct a lady on—"

"Sir, you are exactly that rag-mannered! And, believe me, I understand you well enough. It may interest you to know, Mr. Montgomery, that I am four-and-twenty, and Mr. Vinton and Mr. Thorne are not the first gentlemen to come in my way. Nor, I daresay, will they be the last."

Charlotte did not bother to add that up to now, the gentlemen who had come in her way had been known to her her entire life. All good, honest countrymen, they did not act at all like rakes or roués. Nor, for that matter, did any of them go out of their way to pay her compliments or seek her company.

As for what happened today, if she had given it any thought at all, she would have supposed this new turn of events owed less to her charms and more to the matter of supply and demand. As the colonel had pointed out the previous evening, Charlotte was a *young* woman; moreover, she was now the only young woman in the group. In view of such statistics, a female with any claim to common sense did not let a bit of flirtation go to her head.

Even so, Harrison Montgomery had a nerve thinking he could instruct her in proper behavior. The gall of the man!

Thinking only to bring this unpleasant discussion to an end, she said, "Including my brothers, there are now eight males in this group, and of that eight, seven have treated me with the utmost respect. Only one has seen fit to blackmail me, or take me to task over behavior whose impropriety exists only in his head, and we both know the identity of that man! To put it plainly, Mr. Montgomery, I would suggest you not judge all men by your own low standards."

"My own low—" Harrison could not believe the ungrateful chit! How dare she take his well-meant advice and turn it against him. Why, most of the females of his acquaintance fairly hung on his every word. "A truly feminine woman would have welcomed counsel from a wiser head."

Her chin lifted in a decidedly unappreciative manner. "And a real gentleman would have kept his opinions to himself. I certainly did not ask for them. And though it is absurd in the extreme, one might almost think you were jealous of Messrs. Vinton and Thorne."

"Jealous! Of all the female vanity! As you seem so

fond of plain speaking, madam, allow me to inform you that whatever those other gentlemen may have in mind, *I* have not the least desire to set up a flirtation with you."

In an instant, her face went a deep pink. "That is not what I meant by your being j—"

"To put it bluntly, Miss Pelham, I am so completely *not* jealous, that if we were marooned on some uninhabited island, and you were the only female within a thousand miles, you would be completely safe from any advances on my part. No, make that ten thousand miles, and you might still rest assured that I would have no designs upon your virtue."

As soon as the words crossed his lips, Harrison wished them back. Unfortunately, like the evils freed from Pandora's box, words, once spoken, were there for all eternity. They could never be unsaid. "Miss Pelham, I beg your—"

He was talking to the trees, for the lady had turned and walked away before he could offer her his apology. And why not? Why should she stay around to be insulted by a man whose opinion she had not sought.

Ten thousand miles. What a thoroughly ungentlemanly thing to say. He must have taken leave of his senses; otherwise, why would he go to such lengths to convince her that he was not jealous. As for not having designs on her virtue, Harrison had no idea why he had said such a thing. Why would a man feel it necessary to mention his *not* having designs on the virtue of a woman? Especially a woman he most definitely did not wish to bed?

Benizur had been correct, Jonathan Whoever-He-Was kept his own counsel. When the ramblers took

their midday respite, deciding upon a hillside spot
that had them sitting at different levels, overlooking
yet another beautiful wooded valley, Harrison made
a point of selecting a boulder close to the young man.
His hope was that a casual remark here, a deftly
asked inquiry there, would put all his doubts to rest.
Unfortunately, no matter how subtle his questions to
the lad about his family, Jonathan never gave anything away.

Damnation! Harrison had now spoken to both lads,
and he was not the least bit closer to discovering
which of them might be his brother. Both were
bright, likeable, unspoiled young men, and with their
coloring either of them could be Timmy.

Deciding he was being too subtle with his ques-
tioning, Harrison tried a different tack. "I have a
brother myself."

"Have you, sir? Is he older or younger than you?"

"Younger. In fact he is about your age. Fifteen,
is it?"

"Yes, sir."

Ah, they were getting some place at last! "And
Peter? How old is he?"

"Peter is—"

"Andrew!" the younger Mr. Vinton yelled from
farther up the hillside. "Come up here. Miss Pelham
has consented to show me another of her woodland
tricks."

"Famous," his brother yelled back, losing no time
in setting his haversack aside and scurrying up the
fifteen yards or so to where his fellow ramblers were
disposing themselves around their leader.

"You will want to go up as well," Jonathan said.
"M'sister knows all manner of interesting things."

Harrison hesitated. After all, Miss Pelham was
angry with him. She had once told him that if given
the opportunity she might push him off a mountain

and leave him there for the buzzards, and that was *before* he had insulted her. He had assumed it was an idle threat, but considering how angry she had been at their last meeting, he might be wise not to risk it. "Perhaps I will just stay right here," he said, "and rest."

"As you wish, sir."

Only after the young man had begun to scramble up the hillside did Harrison realize he had let Jonathan get away before he discovered any pertinent information. "Damnation," he muttered. If this went on much longer, he would be obliged to confess who he was and just ask outright which one of the lads might be his brother, Timmy.

"Still no success?" Lady Griswall asked.

Harrison had not realized there was anyone close enough to hear him. "I beg your ladyship's pardon for the profanity. I thought I was alone."

"Which is why, I suppose, you wish to find a certain young man. So you need be alone no longer."

That was not what he had meant, but he did not bother to correct her. Instead, much to his surprise, he found himself moving over to where the older lady sat, the last of her tea growing cold in the shallow drinking bowl.

"Money," she began without preamble, "can be both a blessing and a curse. It gives one freedom from worry about the basic necessities. However, it robs one of the freedom to trust other people's motives. The more money involved, the greater the doubt."

Her blue eyes showed an unexpected sadness, and Harrison wondered who had taught her the lesson about money. "Did he break your heart, ma'am?"

For an instant, her eyebrows lifted, as if she was surprised by the question; then she smiled, albeit wistfully. "I thought so at the time. For months I moped about, certain my heart was broken and that I would never love again."

"And did you?"

She smiled in answer and brushed aside a lock of salt-and-pepper hair that had come loose from the braids that circled her head. "It was my nineteenth birthday, and my mother insisted I accompany her and my sister to the local assembly rooms. I was sitting beside a potted palm, enjoying my misery, when a tall, handsome young man walked into the assembly rooms. It was Lord Griswall, and the instant I saw him, I tumbled into love."

"And you forgot the other one?"

"What other one?" she asked, and they both laughed.

They sat in companionable silence for a time; then she said, "I perfectly understand, sir, why you wish to keep secret the object of your quest. There are those who would gladly mold themselves to fit the image of a wealthy man's brother. A nabob's heir, as it were. This said, I have observed both the two lads professing to be Miss Pelham's younger brothers. They are fine young men, and I cannot believe either of them would claim to be what he is not. No matter the money."

"I tend to agree with you, ma'am. Still, I had hoped to have some sort of proof before I made my relationship known."

After a momentary silence, her ladyship said, "Dear Lord Griswall was forever teasing me about my penchant for those lurid marble-board novels."

"Was he?" Harrison asked, puzzled by the apparent non sequitur.

"Invariably," her ladyship continued, "in those stories, when an heir is missing, his identity is eventually proven because he possesses the family birthmark. What of your brother? Had your family the foresight to pass along such an indisputable mark?"

Harrison shook his head. "Remiss of us, I know, but there it is."

"And no scars, I suppose?"

Again, Harrison shook his head. "None that I recall."

Moments later, much to his surprise, he did remember something. The morning of his fifteenth birthday—the day his stepfather took Harrison to Bristol and handed him over to the captain of the Indiaman—Timmy had fallen off his wooden rocking horse and cut himself behind his left ear. The wound had bled profusely, and once Nanny Clark had stanched the bleeding she had put a court plaster on it.

Later that same morning, when Harrison was sitting in the carriage, his stepfather occupying the forward-facing seat, Nanny Clark had defied orders and brought Timmy out to the carriageway to wave good-bye. She held the three-year-old in her arms, the plaster appearing overly large on Timmy's small neck.

"Good-bye, Master Sonny," his old nurse called, before hiding her face behind her handkerchief.

" 'Bye, Sonny," Timmy called; then he, too, burst into tears.

That was the last time Harrison saw Timmy or Nanny Clark. By the time he returned to England, both his mother and Nanny Clark lay in the churchyard, and Timmy was gone.

Could there have been a scar? Excited at the thought that there might actually be some way of identifying his brother, Harrison excused himself to Lady Griswall and made his way up the hillside where Jonathan sat with the rest of the group, who were listening to Charlotte Pelham. Hoping to sneak a look behind the lad's left ear, he sat just up the hill from the boy and watched his every move, waiting for the opportune moment.

"Actually," Miss Pelham said, "there is an even easier way to tell the time."

"Famous," the younger Mr. Vinton said. "Will you show us, ma'am?"

"Of course. First, you locate the sun, being careful to shield your eyes from its harsh rays; then you find the horizon just below it."

Without prompting, everyone searched out the sun and the horizon, as she instructed. When all of them were looking heavenward, she continued. "Hold one of your hands at the line of the horizon, palm toward you."

"Right or left?" young Vinton asked.

"It does not matter," she replied patiently. "Now, in the manner of one building a stone wall, stack one hand on top of the other—palms still facing you—until the final hand reaches the bottom of the sun. You count the number of hands needed as you go. Each hand is the equivalent of an hour. If it is morning, the tally represents the number of hours since dawn. If it is afternoon, the total represents the number of hours before darkness falls."

While everyone counted their stacked hands, Harrison tried to get a look at Jonathan's neck, just behind his left ear. If there was a scar, the lad's thick, slightly longish hair covered it. Though a bit disappointed, Harrison was not discouraged.

It was altogether possible that the fall off the rocking horse had not left a scar. Still, this was the first lead Harrison had had, and he had no intention of giving up after only one try.

He was just wondering how best to pursue the matter when Mr. Andrew Vinton let out a yell. "My haversack!"

He had left his haversack where he had sat to have his meal, and now the canvas was sliding down the hillside on its way to the valley below. Naturally, all the males jumped up to give chase, leaving Miss Pelham quite alone, and once they were all too far away to hear what was being said, Harrison took the opportunity to see if he could make amends to the lady for both his unsolicited advice and his ungentlemanly remarks.

"Miss Pelham," he said, moving to stand a foot or so from where she sat, "may I speak with you?"

She nodded her head in acquiescence, but the look she turned on Harrison was cold enough to freeze seawater. "What is it, Mr. Montgomery?"

"I was wondering, Miss Pelham, if you have had much experience with donkeys?"

"Donkeys?" Though her tone was still cool, her eyes betrayed her, and Harrison could tell she was intrigued by the question.

"Once," she began, "when I was a little girl, my family went on holiday to Brighton. As you may know, they have donkeys for hire on the beach there, and when I saw them, I asked my father if I might ride one. At first Papa refused, telling me that I would not enjoy the experience, but when I begged, he finally gave me the sixpence required and told me to do as I wished."

"So you had your ride."

"I did not. As usual, my father was in the right of it, for when I got close enough to see the poor creatures—the way they were overused, underfed, and often beaten with a stick to combat their naturally obstinate nature—I did not have the heart to add to their burden by taking my turn on their backs."

She blushed as if embarrassed to have admitted to a bit of compassion. "Now, Mr. Montgomery, allow me to ask why you brought up the subject of donkeys."

"The answer to that should be obvious, ma'am, considering the inflexibility of their nature."

"Perhaps it should. Unfortunately, I—"

"About an hour ago, Miss Pelham, I behaved like a complete jackass, and I was hoping that if you had much experience with the breed, you might consider the source and forgive me for what was inexcusable behavior."

To Harrison's relief, her lips twitched. "I will take it under advisement, sir, and let you know my decision later."

"How much later?"

"Hmm. Impatient as well as intractable."

"Guilty as charged, ma'am."

She held her hand up toward the sky, palm toward her. "I will give you my decision, sir, when the sun is one hand's width from the horizon."

Chapter Eight

Windermere, the largest of the finger lakes, boasted long stretches of beach and truly breathtaking scenery, and had time allowed it, Charlotte would have liked nothing better than to spend a few days there. The inn was delightful enough to make any traveler wish to linger, with its red sandstone mullioned windows and its dark oak ceiling beams, and the food served them in the large, well-appointed private dining parlor was marvelous, especially so to ramblers who had worked up rather impressive appetites.

With such taste-tempting delights as onion soup, removed for a dressed breast of lamb, a fricassee of turnip, and a ragout of celery in wine sauce, everyone in the group, even the still slightly ill Wilfred Bryce, ate heartily. As for the trifle containing at least six different fruits and accompanied by a platter of the thickly sliced local cheese, that sumptuous dish was such a success that nothing would do Colonel Fitzgibbon but to venture personally to the kitchen to extend his compliments to the chef.

Once the dessert and cheese were finished, Charlotte and Lady Griswall left the gentlemen to their port and cigars. After draping their shawls over their bare arms to ward off the evening chill, the ladies went out onto the cobbled terrace to admire the moonlight that shimmered silvery white on the surface of the dark blue water. The inn had been built on the hillside, where it nestled beneath the slopes of Touhrigg Fell, and though it was nowhere near as dramatically situated as Ghyll Inn, it had its own drama, beginning with the mellowed stone steps—at least fifty of them—that led from the terrace down to the sandy shores of Lake Windermere.

"What a romantic picture," Charlotte said. "It fairly tempts one to float down those starlit steps in hopes of finding some handsome knight on a white horse waiting at the water's edge."

"I feel no such temptation," her ladyship replied. "As for me, should I be inclined to go in search of knights—handsome or otherwise—I would much prefer the more prosaic footpath that winds its way through the trees just yonder."

"But, ma'am, the steps are so, so . . ."

"Treacherous?" Harrison Montgomery supplied for her from the doorway.

Charlotte was thankful for the cloak of darkness, for she was embarrassed at having been caught speaking romantic nonsense. "Actually, sir, I was thinking the steps were rather magical."

"Magical until one tripped, Miss Pelham, and tumbled down several dozen of those bone crushers to land at that young Lancelot's feet. Take my word for it, bruises are not at all romantic. I know, because I have had a million of them. Furthermore, we males are virtually worthless when it comes to tending the injured, not to mention being notoriously fickle."

"Fickle?"

"Without question. Fall at his feet, madam, and quick as you can say, 'Bob's your uncle,' that knight will jump on his trusty charger and flee with all speed. No doubt in search of a damsel who plays at being hard to get."

Though she had laughed, her ladyship said, "You

are rather harsh in your judgment of your own sex, Mr. Montgomery."

"Not at all, ma'am. Donkeys, the lot of us."

He waited a fraction of a second, then added, "Speaking of donkeys reminds me, Miss Pelham, of your experience at Brighton. You told me you would not ride the poor, mistreated creatures for hire there, and because I seem to remember hearing *one* of your brothers say that you were an excellent horsewoman, I wondered if you had ever ridden anything more exotic than a horse."

"Not unless a sheepdog qualifies as exotic."

Harrison could not suppress a chuckle. "I collect, ma'am, that this experience was some time ago."

"Oh, quite twenty years ago, I am sure. Though now that I think about it, since my nurse dragged me off the poor dog before I had been on its back for more than a matter of seconds, I suppose it does not qualify as a bona fide ride."

Harrison smiled at the picture in his mind of a small, intrepid girl in short skirts and high-buttoned shoes, throwing a chubby leg over a startled sheepdog. Well, perhaps she had not possessed chubby legs, but he would bet a golden guinea she had been intrepid.

"However," she continued, "if the opportunity should ever come my way, I should like to ride a camel."

Intrepid to the bone! "One hump, Miss Pelham, or two?"

Charlotte knew he was teasing her, but she did not really mind. True, she had been furious with him earlier, and not a little mortified to be told that if she were the only woman within ten thousand miles, he would still not wish to pursue her. However, he had apologized most handsomely for his rudeness, and she had finally forgiven him. Now, it appeared he was making an effort to win her friendship.

"Definitely two humps," she said. "The kind one sees in paintings of Egypt. I understand the Egyptians even have camel races."

"So I have heard. I have never traveled to Egypt, of course, so I have no experience of camels, but I have traveled by elephant on more than one occasion."

"By elephant! How marvelous. Tell me, if you please, what is it like being atop such a large animal?"

Her enthusiasm was contagious, and Harrison was obliged to smile. "Like nothing else I have ever experienced."

"Oh, no, sir. That will not do. You cannot offer me up an elephant story, then attempt to fob me off with generalities. I want details."

More than willing to comply, he said, "The closest I can describe it is like sitting atop a moving mountain."

Several other of the gentlemen had found their way onto the terrace by this time, and Mr. Andrew Vinton feigned interest in the conversation, using it as an excuse to join the three of them. "Forgive the intrusion," he said, stopping so close to Miss Pelham their shoulders almost touched. "Pray continue, Montgomery. You find me positively agog to hear more of your experience with the elephants."

Harrison knew a rather primitive desire to land the solicitor a facer. Whether the desire stemmed from the fellow's condescending tone to him to continue, or from his presuming he might join Miss Pelham with impunity, Harrison could not say.

"May we join, too?" young Jonathan asked, pulling his supposed brother along with him.

Harrison stepped back, making room for the two

lads, all the while wishing the moon was bright enough to show him the backs of their necks. "I was about to explain to your sister that most of the Europeans who choose to travel by elephant content themselves with sitting in the howdah, which is a covered settee attached to a saddlelike platform."

"But not you?" Peter asked, his excited face begging Harrison to agree that it was so.

"Guilty as charged."

"I knew it!" the lad all but shouted. "Do you ride bareback, sir? As the Indians do?"

"Actually, one rides not on the animal's back, but on its shoulders. And a less comfortable experience I cannot describe. Especially when the flies are heavy and the elephant constantly flaps its leathery ears to shoo them away. Since the rider's limbs are just behind those large ears, the result for the unwary is not unlike that of being flogged with a cat-o'-nine-tails."

"Even so," Jonathan said, "I wager you wouldn't keep m'sister in that howdah thing for very long."

"Right you are," Peter added. "What say you, Charlie? Do you think you could stay on an elephant's neck?"

"Perhaps not. But I should certainly like to give it a try."

Harrison was not the least bit surprised by her reply. "Be warned, Miss Pelham, it is rather a rough ride. One must learn to relax the knees and roll with the pachyderm's gait, and the result is sometimes a feeling not unlike seasickness. As well, when one sits so high off the ground, the inclines can be scary. Especially since elephants tend to take the truly steep hills by sliding down them on their bellies."

"Truly? On their bellies?"

"I fear so, ma'am. And even grown men have been known to swoon at such an experience."

"By Jove!" Jonathan said. "Ready to cry craven, Charlie?"

"Not a bit of it," Miss Pelham assured him. "I would still like to climb aboard."

"Tell me," Lady Griswall said, "does the animal really drink using his long nose?"

"It does, ma'am, though the correct term for the appendage is a trunk. And a most inspiring appendage it is. On my first ride, my elephant became alarmed at something, I was never sure what, and after making a sort of grumbling sound in its head, it lifted its trunk way above its head and mine, then emitted a series of trumpets that practically deafened me."

"What an adventure," Peter said. "Should you ever return to India, sir, may I come along?"

"What about me?" Jonathan said.

"And let Jonathan come, too," Peter added.

At the innocent request, memories suddenly flooded Harrison's consciousness—recollections so painfully vivid he could not speak for the obstruction they caused in his throat. The memory was of the day he left for Bristol. When he went up to the nursery to bid Timmy farewell, the little fellow had thrown himself into his big brother's arms and begged him not to go away.

Though Harrison was fifteen years old at the time, far too old to cry, he had felt tears sting his eyes. "Sorry, old fellow," he had said. "I do not want to go, but I have no choice in the matter."

"Then take me with you, Sonny," his little brother had begged. "Let me come, too."

Wednesday morning was as gray as the first two days had been glorious, and when the party set out for the first half of the day's journey, the sky was so overcast it was impossible to see the beautiful fells to the west. As if taking their cue from the somber sky, the walkers did not indulge in their usual banter, and before they reached Staveley, the rains came. And what rains they were!

After years in India, where long periods of drought—drought that left the baked earth criss-crossed with long, wide fissures—were followed by monsoons that lasted so long a person could go mad for want of a dry spot to sit, Harrison had forgotten the intensity of English rains.

A chill breeze had been at their backs all morning, making Harrison grateful for the thick seaman's jacket Benizur had purchased the day before. When the breeze became a wind, the slightly faded wool was most welcome, and as the gusts gained momentum, Harrison turned up the collar of the jacket to protect his ears. Minutes later, the wind was joined by large, cold raindrops that pelted the walkers like a barrage of pebbles thrown by mischievous boys.

Like the others, Harrison quickly retrieved the oiled cloth from his haversack, removed his slouch hat, then slipped his head through the slit in the cloth. The makeshift rain gear, which would double as ground cover should they wish to sleep out-of-doors, covered him to midthigh, and for a time it served to protect him. Before he knew what was happening, however, thunderclaps began to rumble in the distance. Unfortunately, the thunder lost no time in moving closer, and as it traveled their way, those cold raindrops increased in number and finally merged into a solid sheet of water—water that was bone chilling and unrelenting in its assault upon the heads and shoulders of the miserable humans.

As leader of the group, Charlotte felt it behooved her to maintain as positive an outlook as possible. As the rain continued, however, the day's fifteen miles felt more like twenty-five, and her spirits began to droop as badly as the felt brim of her hat. When the brim finally became completely saturated and collapsed, allowing the rainwater to flow from the crown of the hat directly into her coat collar, Charlotte decided she had been positive long enough. "Devil take it," she muttered.

"Did you say something?" someone shouted from behind her.

She turned to discover Harrison Montgomery, whose hat, like hers, had given way and was allowing rain inside his newly acquired jacket. The man was a marvel, for each day he produced another article of clothing to replace the totally unsuitable clothes he had worn on the first day. Expensive, well-made walking boots had appeared as if by magic, and now a wool seaman's jacket. What next? Rabbits out of his hat?

Unwilling to tell him that she was wishing herself inside, next to a warm fire, she attempted a smile. "No doubt this rain has helped to restore your memory of our changeable English weather."

"Quite," he said. "I also recalled, Miss Pelham, that when we spoke the other day, you called the weather fickle."

"I believe that was the word I used."

"Then may I suggest that when we reach the next inn, you inquire if the landlord has one of Mr. Johnson's lexicons?"

The day was gray, the wind and rain miserably cold, and yet Charlotte felt herself smile. "And why should I have need of a lexicon?"

He rubbed his hand across his face in a vain attempt to stem the constant flow of water. "Because 'fickle' does not come close to describing this weather."

"Oh? And what word would you use?"

He smiled then, and for an instant Charlotte felt

as if the sun shone. "Demonic," he said. "Indisputably demonic."

Though she quite agreed with him, she made no reply; she simply turned and continued to walk. Needless to say, she was as happy as the rest of the party to see the Skelwith Inn at Staveley. Though the miserable weather had its effect upon the inn's gray stone, giving it the appearance of a haunted mansion lifted from the pages of one of Mrs. Edgeworth's gothic novels, Charlotte hurried across the muddy inn yard and pushed open the heavily studded oak door.

"Tea," she said, the moment she spied Jonathan in conversation with the landlord, "and plenty of it. And see how quickly the kitchen can furnish hot water to the various rooms."

Though the rain did not abate for three solid days, the ramblers voted to continue their journey. Andrew Vinton and Wilfred Bryce were on holiday and were obliged to return to their respective positions in the City, and Lawrence Vinton needed to return to Oxford to resume his studies. As well, Lady Griswall was promised at a house party the first weekend in June.

"It is at Oatlands," she explained to the group, "and I cannot miss it. Otherwise, I would have been quite happy to remain in this comfortable establishment for as long as need be."

"No, no," the colonel agreed, obviously impressed by the very mention of the country home of the Duke and Duchess of York. "Must not insult the royals."

"It is not a matter of insult," she explained to Charlotte later, "for the duchess is the kindest of souls, and almost never takes offense. Unless, of course, one is so foolish as to snub one of her numerous dogs, which, I assure you, Miss Pelham, I would never do. I like animals. Well, not snakes," she said, grimacing at the thought, "or lizards, for that matter, but I am inordinately fond of hounds, and I would never be unkind to one."

"Of course you would not, ma'am. Nor is there any need for you to miss the duchess's house party. Not if it can be helped. And, since the vote was unanimous for us to continue as planned, I will do all within my power to see that we arrive at Robin's Hood Bay on the appointed day."

"You are very good, Miss Pelham. If I had been blessed with a daughter, which, unfortunately I was not, I should have been pleased if she had possessed your spirit of adventure, coupled with your pretty, unaffected ways."

Much touched by the sincere and very flattering compliment, Charlotte thanked her ladyship and asked if she would be so kind as to call her by her first name.

"A pleasure, my dear Charlotte."

After the initial vote, there was no further discussion about not keeping to the schedule, and the only concession their guide made to the weather was in avoiding the hillier routes and choosing instead to lead the party over the old mule trails that zigzagged through the last of the Lake District. By the sixth day, as they crossed the usually pretty Eden River—which was now muddy and roiling—and continued onward toward the Pennines, the rain slowly abated.

In deference to the Sabbath, the group did not travel on Sunday; instead, they remained two nights at a pleasant inn that was an old converted priory, enjoying a much-needed respite from the wet. With little to do except stay in their respective rooms and nap, or go to the common room, with its huge fire-place, to read or play cards, the three younger members of the party began to grow restive.

"If I am obliged to sit through another rubber of whist," Jonathan whispered to Charlotte as she and Lady Griswall rose from the dinner table Sunday evening, "I vow I will go mad. Can you think of nothing we might do?"

"I make no promises," she whispered back, "but I will give it some thought."

"Bless you," he said, no longer bothering to keep his voice low. "Were it not for her ladyship, you would be my favorite female on this walk."

"Some compliments," Lady Griswall said, giving him a look that was a fine blend of reprimand and unconcealed pleasure, "are best kept to oneself."

Charlotte, not the least offended, advised her ladyship to pay him no heed. "For I assure you I do not."

"Perhaps you share my opinion," Mr. Andrew Vinton said, his tone unmistakably flirtatious, "that all younger brothers should be bound and gagged until they are at least one-and-twenty."

Mr. Lawrence Vinton murmured some sort of brotherly demur, but his remark was covered by that of Mr. Wilfred Bryce, who bowed first to Lady Griswall, then to Charlotte. "If I may be allowed to contradict Miss Pelham's young relative, both the ladies are much to be admired."

It was all Charlotte could do to stifle a groan, for Mr. Bryce had outdone himself during the afternoon, toadying to Lady Griswall at every opportunity. Each suit she took while at the card table was occasion for applause, and her opinions on every subject, no matter how trivial, were seconded, then repeated, until Charlotte thought she might be tempted to drown the clerk at the first suitable river.

Thankfully, she was not obliged to suffer his conversation after dinner, for when the gentlemen exited the small dining parlor and joined the ladies in the common room, he went immediately to the card table, where he was joined by Colonel Fitzgibbon, Mr. Thorne, and the older Mr. Vinton.

Mr. Montgomery very politely asked the ladies if they would like to make up a second table for silver loo, and when they both declined, he declared himself just as happy to join them by the fire. "A relaxing evening would not come amiss."

As if in definition of the word "relaxing," he rested his right shoulder against the oversize oak mantelpiece and crossed one elegantly booted foot over the other. Gone were the heavy walking boots and the wet wool sailor's jacket, and in their place he wore a beautifully tailored coat of sable brown superfine, with an ivory waistcoat and York tan breeches. Because the group did not stand on ceremony when dressing for dinner, the gentleman was suitably attired for an afternoon drive in the park.

The mellowed ivory of his waistcoat seemed to accent his sun-bronzed skin, and the snug fit of his breeches served to emphasize the power and strength of his lower limbs. Though much had passed between Charlotte and Harrison Montgomery since the first day she saw him climb down from his Tilbury, she still thought him unquestionably the most impressive man she had ever seen. Breathtakingly impressive.

To turn her thoughts from his magnificent physique, she informed him that if a peaceful evening was what he desired, then he had best retire to the far end of the room. "For you must know, sir, that I have promised the three younger members of the party a bit of foolishness. Beginning with something the landlord's grandchildren left here some time back."

"Grandchildren?" Harrison asked.

The lady had been hiding something beneath the Norwich shawl she wore over a China crepe dinner dress of a most becoming peach color, and now she pushed the shawl aside to reveal a small cloth bag with a drawstring closure. "Marbles," she said.

"Oh, Lord!" Jonathan said, upon entering the common room and seeing the little cloth bag. "She's got marbles, Peter."

His supposed brother groaned; then the two of them began immediately to warn Lawrence Vinton against even *trying* to best Charlotte at spans-and-snops or bost-about. "Of course, you may have a chance at knock-out or ringtaw," Peter graciously conceded, "but only if you are truly accomplished."

As it turned out, none of the three were quite as accomplished as Miss Charlotte Pelham. Shouts, groans, and name-calling had become the order of the day, and after a truly boisterous hour spent on the floor playing at least seven of the nine marble games they knew, the three young men were obliged to admit defeat at the lady's hands.

"I told you how it would be," Jonathan said. "M'sister never loses."

"It is all the result of Miss Pelham's much smaller hands," Lawrence Vinton said. "Mine have grown too big to allow me to release the marbles with anything like the dexterity I had a few years ago. Otherwise, I might have shown her a thing or two."

Naturally, the young man's two companions greeted his excuse with a chorus of hoots and hisses, and when the undisputed champion bid them show a bit of consideration for Mr. Vinton's feelings, the rude noises were turned her way. Obviously inured to such behavior, she merely laughed them off, and when she gathered up the hem of her skirt in preparation to stand, Harrison left his place beside the mantel, reached down, and took her hands.

"Allow me," he said, pulling her to her feet.

To his surprise, her hands *were* small and amazingly soft. And as he held them in his, absently rubbing his thumbs over the skin that covered the fine bones, a most unwelcome question sprang to his mind, a question regarding the possible softness hidden beneath the peach-colored China crepe.

He tried to turn his thoughts in a more decorous direction, but his brain would not cooperate. It did not help him in the least that the lady's cheeks were becomingly pink from sitting close to the fire, and that her eyes were still alight with the fun of the childish game she had entered into with such relish. As well, the Norwich shawl had slipped off her shoulders, exposing a totally feminine swell of bosom revealed by the low neckline of her dress.

Had there not been eight other people in the room, Harrison was quite certain he would have bent his head to taste her smiling lips. Thankfully, there were others present, so such action was out of the question. Thinking he might be well advised to step out-of-doors and let the icy rain cool him off, he let go of the lady's hands and stepped back.

Charlotte had allowed Mr. Montgomery to assist her to rise, and like that other time he had lifted her off the ground, the experience had left her a bit breathless. He was very strong, and his hands, which were as bronzed as his face, were warm and slightly rough, with long, tapered fingers and just a sprinkle of fine, light brown hair showing at his thick wrists.

"Your hands *are* small," he said softly, and though Lawrence Vinton had made much the same observation moments earlier, that young gentleman's remark had occasioned not the least response in Charlotte.

When Harrison Montgomery said it, however, the words left her tingling all over.

Though she was certain he was unaware of what he was doing, the gentleman rubbed his thumbs across her knuckles, causing a warmth that started somewhere in her midsection and radiated to even the most secret places of her body. To her surprise, it crossed her mind that had he given her just the least encouragement, she would have stood on tiptoes and offered him her lips to kiss.

Thankfully, before she had the opportunity to act upon such a brazen notion, she remembered what he had said just a few days ago about her being completely safe from any advances on his part. "If you were the only female within a thousand miles," he had said. "No, ten thousand."

She was safe from his advances. If he had written his feelings in a letter and posted it to her, his meaning could not have been plainer. He did not find her attractive. Not in the least.

Now, as Harrison Montgomery released her hands and stepped back, Charlotte mentally consigned to perdition those perverse fates who had seen fit to make her so powerfully drawn to a man who found nothing whatever to like about her.

Chapter Nine

"Well?" Benizur asked, handing him the heavy boots that had sat beside the bedchamber stove for two days drying out. "Which one has the scar?"

Harrison managed to avoid the canny man's far-too-observant eyes, for he had no wish to explain that he had forgotten all about checking out the necks of Jonathan and Peter Whoever-They-Were. He had had an excellent opportunity, standing at the fireplace while the two lads sat on the floor playing marbles, and yet, he had not taken advantage of that occasion. In truth, once the foursome was on the floor, Harrison's mind had been elsewhere.

How could he have forgotten? What sort of man did that make him? His only reason for being there was to discover which of those young men might be his brother. That was his quest, the most important thing in his life, and yet he had spent the better part of the evening watching Charlotte Pelham, and the better part of the night imagining her rounded bosom pressed against his naked chest.

"I could not see their necks," he said. Of course he could not, for he had been distracted by Miss Pelham's warm skin. And her chocolate brown eyes. And her smiling lips. And . . .

"Will you wear the knife today?" Benizur asked.

Brought back to the present, Harrison nodded. He

took the tooled leather sheath containing the slim, deceptively innocent-looking blade, then slipped his left arm though the leather string Benizur had run through the slits in the sheath. Once the weapon was close against his ribs, concealed beneath his waist-coat, he slipped on the thick seaman's jacket.

"Today is Peter's day to drive the wagon," he said, "and I have every intention of staying close to young Jonathan during the entire walk."

"A good plan, Sahib."

Monday was the eighth day of their journey, and though the sky had appeared leaden when they first left the old converted priory, by midmorning the rain had ended altogether and the sun began making in-termittent forays from behind the lingering clouds.

Still, the walkers kept to the less-demanding trails, leaving the more adventurous route until the ground had sufficient time to dry. "I should not like to see anyone take a bad spill," Charlotte said just before they left the inn.

"A good plan," Mr. Thorne agreed.

Since those were the exact words Benizur had used, Harrison remembered his own plan and dropped back so he might walk with Jonathan.

He began his inquisition casually enough by men-tioning the marbles the three young gentlemen had played with Charlotte last evening. "I enjoyed watch-ing the games. It has been so long since I played, I had forgotten many of the rules and strategies."

"You should have joined us, sir. Would have been most welcome, I assure you."

Harrison smiled his thanks. The lads were well brought up; someone had paid close attention to their morals and their manners. Both boys showed respect for their elders without ever being in the least fawning, and they had an easy, yet loving relationship with Charlotte.

As much as it pained him to realize it, his younger brother was probably a better person for having been reared by strangers. Though, of course, they were only strangers to Harrison. Strangers who probably would resent Harrison's coming into Timmy's life, wanting to spend time with him, and possibly upsetting the established pattern of their family as they had known it for eleven years.

"I understand," he began again, "that you and Peter were at Eton."

"Yes, sir."

"I have not seen the school since I went to sea twelve years ago. I should imagine it has changed."

"I cannot think it has, for Hough, my best friend other than Peter, was visited several times by his uncle, who had been at Eton himself eons ago. According to Hough's uncle, the place had not changed by so much as a blade of grass."

Talk of Eton finally led to a discussion of Jonathan's future plans.

"I want to go up to Cambridge," he said. "Peter and I both want to go."

"What is preventing you?" Hoping a lighter tone might keep his questions from sounding as officious as they actually were, he said, "Never tell me the two of you are a pair of dunces."

"Oh, no, sir. Peter took a double first and I—"

"And you?" Harrison prompted.

"And I talk far too much. Forgive me, sir, for being such a bore. You cannot want to be listening to me forever prosing on about myself."

It was exactly what he wanted, but sensing a bit of reserve creeping into the lad's manner, Harrison wisely let the matter drop for the moment. Time enough to speak to him again after the noon break.

For now, he would move on ahead before the boy became suspicious of his motives. "I was not in the least bored," he said, "but I see Lady Griswall just ahead, and there is something I wish to ask her. If you will excuse me?"

"Of course," Jonathan said, his manner relaxing once again. "A fine old girl is Lady B. Not a bit starched up." He lowered his voice. "Don't mind confiding to you, sir, that m'sister was a bit nervous when she first discovered that one of the aristocracy would be joining the tour."

"Miss Pelham afraid of anything? I cannot credit it. Why, should we encounter a Bengal tiger along the way, I would expect your sister to box his ears and send him on his way."

"As to that," the lad said, a smile on his open, still-boyish face, "Charlie could probably hold her own with a tiger. But," he added, the smile fading, "she would have been hurt if the ladies on the tour had decided to snub her, her seeking employment and all. And if they had treated her coldly, there would not have been a thing Peter or I could have done about it."

"Oh, yes," her ladyship replied, "Charlotte is a dear girl, and both the lads are protective of her. Just the sort of young men to make any mother proud. Or any brother."

The noon break had come and gone, and Harrison and her ladyship were up front on the path, with the rest of the ramblers following their lead, and Miss Pelham bringing up the rear. Harrison was looking skyward, enjoying what he hoped would be a permanent reappearance of the sun, when the path turned sharply and her ladyship gasped, then stopped suddenly, as if unwilling to move another step.

"Oh," she said. "Oh, dear. Oh, dear me."

He looked first at the lady, whose kind, plain face had turned ashen; then he turned toward the object of her rather wide-eyed stare, a large, flat rock some three feet away. "What is it, ma'am? Are you in pain? Are you unwell?"

"No, no," she said, her voice becoming more tremulous by the moment. "It is just—" She appeared unable to say more, and merely pointed instead, in the direction of the rock.

Since her feet seemed firmly planted on the still-muddy trail, Harrison moved toward the rock to see what had upset her, covering the short distance in only a second or two. If he had been a moment slower, he would have missed seeing the small adder that slithered off the rock, where it had been sunning, to hide beneath a mound of tussock grass just beyond. Naturally, the reptile was more frightened of the giant in the heavy boots than Harrison was of it, but he sympathized with Lady Griswall's fear.

In India, where snakes were numerous, the people learned to live in relative harmony with the creatures. The opposite was true in England, however, where untold numbers of people had never even seen a snake. In general, if an Englishman encountered a reptile, his fear of the unknown prompted him to kill the poor creature on sight.

Harrison was standing there, wondering what was best to do, when Mr. Thorne approached him slowly. "Is it an adder?" he asked.

"Yes. Just there, behind the tussock grass."

Remembering the laugh he and the ladies had enjoyed at Thorne's expense over the matter of the mouse and the stolen stocking, Harrison was not a little surprised at the birder's sensible approach to the problem.

"One tends to see them more at this time of year.

Adders, I mean, for they have not been out of their winter hibernation for long. I daresay that little fellow was merely trying to warm up after the recent cold and rainy days. It would be a shame to kill him for no reason. Do you not agree?"

"Wholeheartedly. But what do we do about her ladyship? She is quite distressed."

Mr. Thorne was silent for a moment, apparently considering the problem. "Would it serve, do you think, if one of us carried her past the spot, while the other watched to see that the reptile did not move from its hiding place? If she has no reason to fear personal contact with the snake, she might feel more comfortable about letting the poor little fellow live."

Harrison studied the blond gentleman. Though Thorne was quite fit, and possessed of the lean, hard muscles of the seasoned rock climber, Harrison could give him at least five inches in height and outweighed him a good three stone. "You watch the snake, Thorne. I will inquire if Lady Griswall will agree to let me carry her."

The lady agreed to the plan, apparently pleased with any suggestion that got her feet off the same ground inhabited by the reptile. Harrison had only just scooped her into his arms when the other ramblers came around the turn in the trail.

The colonel was the first to see them. "I say, Montgomery. Has her ladyship fallen? Not injured a limb, I hope?"

Harrison was about to answer when he saw Charlotte coming forward, maneuvering around the others at a brisk pace. "Excuse me, let me pass."

"Keep everyone else here," he said to the colonel, "and give Miss Pelham a few minutes alone with Lady Griswall. Mr. Thorne will explain everything after we leave."

Charlotte had heard Mr. Montgomery's instruction,

and whatever may have happened, it sounded like an excellent plan of action to her. She started to take the lead when the gentleman caught her arm to stop her. "Walk behind me," he said.

It was an order, clear and simple, but unsure what had happened, she decided it would be foolish to waste time arguing the point of who was in charge. "As you wish, sir."

As they began to walk, her ladyship wound her arms rather tightly around Mr. Montgomery's neck and hid her face in his shoulder. "I . . . I am so sorry, sir. This is unforgivably foolish, I know, but . . . but . . ."

"Shh," he said softly, the sound meant more for comfort than admonition. "Just think of something pleasant, ma'am, and like Aladdin's magic carpet, I will whisk you to a place where you will feel more comfortable."

When they passed Mr. Thorne, who kept his attention fastened on a clump of tussock grass, Charlotte formed a pretty good notion of what had happened. Lady Griswall had confided to her that she was afraid of snakes and lizards, and whichever of those creatures she had spied, the experience had given her a genuine fright.

Mr. Montgomery carried the frightened lady for perhaps half a mile, all the while speaking in a soft, soothing tone, telling her something or other about the brilliance of the sunsets in the Southern Hemisphere, and while they walked, Charlotte searched out a sturdy birch limb. Finding one that was about four feet long and reasonably straight, she broke it off and began to remove the new silvery green leaves.

When the gentleman found a spot that was both flat enough and open enough to afford her ladyship a comfortable view of her surroundings, he asked if

she was ready for the magic carpet to land. She nodded, and while he continued to talk soothing nonsense to her, he set her on her feet, though he kept
his arm securely around her waist.

"If you will, ma'am," Charlotte said, approaching
Lady Griswall, "I got you a sort of shepherd's staff.
Perhaps it will make you feel more secure."

"Just the thing," Harrison said. "And when you
no longer have need of it, ma'am, Charlotte can use
it to beat off her many admirers."

The object of his sally knew he was merely trying
to lift Lady Griswall's spirits, so she took no offense,
merely answered him in kind. "Any more of your
fresh remarks, Mr. Montgomery, and I shall know
upon whom to use that stick."

"Consider me warned, Miss Pelham."

Charlotte. Deuce take it! He had called her by her
name. He had not meant to, of course; it had just
slipped out. Fortunately, neither of the ladies seemed
to notice. Lady Griswall was still too nervous to
know what was being said, and Miss Pelham was
much more concerned with doing all within her power
to see that her ladyship regained her composure.

Which was no less than Harrison had come to expect from their intrepid leader. She was a young lady
of uncommon common sense, and both her heart and
her head were in the right place. Without realizing
he had done so, Harrison had begun to appreciate
those qualities in her.

He walked some distance away, to give the ladies
a few moments of privacy, and when he stopped
near a small, rocky outcropping, he noticed a hopeful
bee buzzing around a lone, bright yellow rockfoil—
saxifrage he thought it was called—that struggled for
a foothold among the rocks. Tenacious both of
them—the flower and the bee. Just like Miss Pelham.

Harrison enjoyed a sweetly scented rose as much

as the next man, but in all fairness, he had to admire the rockfoil—a flower that made its own place in the world, sinking its roots into unfriendly soil, and flourishing in defiance of all logic. And all without depending upon daily pampering by a gardener. Similarly, there was something to be said for a female who took a bit of initiative when it was called for, showed a bit of fortitude under pressure.

How different his life would have been if his and Timmy's mother had been such a female. Had that timid lady possessed even half Miss Pelham's strength, she would never have turned her life and her fortune over to a domineering man like Thomas James. Had Anne Montgomery exhibited just a little courage, stood her ground just once, one of her sons would not have been forced into a life at sea, and her other son would have been reared in his own home, where he belonged.

Harrison could just imagine what Charlotte Pelham would do if someone tried to send her child away. Like a mother tiger defending its cub, she would fight tooth and claw. Had Harrison's mother shown only a fraction of that determination, he would never have been sent from the only home he had ever known, nor would he have lost his little brother, the only person he had ever loved.

Calling himself to task for dwelling on adversities best left in the past, he returned to the ladies, who sat on the ground, apparently lost in quiet conversation. "Do I intrude?" he asked.

"Never," her ladyship replied, an uncertain smile on her lips.

"Please," Charlotte said, "join us."

"I was just wondering, Miss Pelham, if her ladyship was ready to resume the walk. If so, I should be pleased to offer her my arm."

While he reached his hand down to help Lady

Griswall rise, assuring her as he did so that he would
remain by her side for the rest of the journey, Charlotte scrambled to her feet unassisted. She did not
want Harrison Montgomery to touch her. Not at this
moment. She still felt a bit skittish after her reaction
to him last evening, and today, after witnessing his
tender treatment of Lady Griswall, Charlotte felt doubly vulnerable.

Also, though she had tried not to react, she had
not missed it several minutes ago when he had called
her by her given name. It might well have been a
slip of the tongue, but even so, she had loved hearing
her name on his lips.

Not that it meant anything. After all, the man had
made it perfectly clear how he felt about her. Unfortunately, he seemed to be occupying more and more
of Charlotte's thoughts these past few days, and if
she were not careful, she would end this fortnight
with a broken heart.

The Eagle Inn, their stopover for Monday night,
was a charming hodgepodge of a place, with modern
oriel windows that looked out onto a coach yard surrounded by buildings dating from the early sixteenth
century. The Eagle Inn boasted a quite distinctive
open gallery, and on the fourth Monday of every
month, the local assemblies were held there.

To the delight of the ramblers, who were happy
for some new form of activity, May's assembly was
to be held that very night.

"Yes, I know the gentlemen are going," Charlotte
told Lady Griswall's maid, who had come to her
room half an hour before they were to go down to
dinner, "but I have nothing suitable to wear to an
assembly."

"But that be why I've come, miss. Her ladyship

bid me inquire if you had brought any garment other than the China crepe you wear for dinner."

Charlotte felt herself blush. The peach-colored crepe had been a birthday gift from her mother, and since it was her newest frock, Charlotte had packed it with confidence. Obviously she had misjudged her needs, for it seemed the other members of the party were growing weary of seeing her in the same dress evening after evening. Slightly embarrassed, and feeling she needed to explain herself, she said, "I packed as lightly as possible."

"Exactly what her ladyship thought you'd say, miss. That be why she bid me tell you she's got a pale cherry satin that would set off your lovely dark hair and eyes to perfection."

Thoroughly embarrassed now, Charlotte shook her head. "I could not possibly—"

"And should you be a-worriting," the servant continued, "I've no doubt the dress will fit you, for as I told her ladyship the last time she wore it, 'My lady,' I said, 'that satin is too snug on you.' It pulls across the bust every time she moves her arms."

The maid looked behind her, as if to make certain no one was listening, though they were alone in Charlotte's bedchamber. "Her ladyship don't like to admit it, but she put on a pound or two while in Lunnon. And at her age, the pounds go on easier than they came off. If I know ought of the matter, she'll never wear that cherry satin again."

Charlotte felt herself relenting. In truth, since she wanted to join the others at the assembly, she was easily persuaded that borrowing an expensive gown was perfectly acceptable behavior. "If you are quite certain."

"Quite certain, miss. Now you just finish with your ablutions, and I'll be back in a few minutes with the dress. And, miss, just brush out your hair, if you please. Leave the dressing of it to me. I've a way with hair, and I've a notion how to do yours up real fine."

Feeling slightly like Cinderella confronted by the fairy godmother, Charlotte did as she was told, and half an hour later, when she went down to dinner, she knew without a doubt that she had never looked better in her entire life.

The cherry satin was expertly cut, with a square neckline and snug-fitting sleeve inserts that reached to her wrists. The gown boasted only one row of frills, and that was at the hem, and the elegant simplicity of the style perfectly suited Charlotte's firm yet rounded figure. She wore no jewelry, having adamantly refused to borrow the diamond necklace Lady Griswall sent to her room.

Actually, Charlotte did not feel she needed any further adornment, not after the maid had put her thick, straight hair into a deceptively simple twist at the nape of her neck. Even in the small looking glass the maid held for her, Charlotte could see that the coiffure gave her neck an elegant, swanlike appearance.

Even without the maid's many compliments and assurances, Charlotte knew she looked beautiful. It was the first time she had ever felt beautiful, and when she entered the private parlor where they were to eat their dinner, the reactions of the gentlemen were everything she could have wanted.

"By Jove, Charlie," Jonathan said upon first spying her, "you look fine as five pence."

"Very nice," Peter added.

"Damned with faint praise," the colonel said, making her a very courtly bow.

For once, Harrison felt he could not have said it better himself! If the truth be known, when the door opened and he had gotten his first look at their guide, he had been struck speechless. As, thankfully, had Mr. Andrew Vinton and Mr. Russell Thorne.

Beautiful did not adequately describe Charlotte Pelham this evening, and for the life of him, Harrison could think of nothing that would fit the bill. Always a pretty girl, tonight she was a diamond of the first water. Exquisite. And if he had the dressing of her, she would always wear vivid colors.

The cherry was perfect with her black hair, which was combed straight back from her face and caught at the nape of her neck with a silver clasp, then arranged in some sort of a twisty thing. It was a simple style, but it suited her to perfection, showing off the soft contours of her face and the long, graceful curve of her neck. An indisputably kissable neck.

As for what the bright satin did for her skin, he did not even try to think of the right words. It was enough that the very sight of her ivory throat and shoulders, left bare by the low cut of the gown, had started a pulse throbbing in his temples—not to mention one or two other places he dared not think about.

"Miss Pelham," Andrew Vinton said, finding his voice at last, "tonight even the angels must be jealous of you." He allowed her no time to respond to his fulsome compliment before he added, "And if I may be so bold, may I claim the first waltz?"

"And the second," Russell Thorne declared, "is mine, fair lady."

Damnation! In that moment, it became startlingly clear to Harrison that he had been remiss in his duties to mankind. He should have murdered those two a sennight ago!

Chapter Ten

Harrison was obliged to wait a full hour before he could claim Charlotte for a dance. Because of the recent bad weather, many of the local ladies had not ventured out that evening, leaving the assembly with an abundance of males, some of them little better than cits. To Harrison's dismay, the master of ceremonies—a jovial fellow with more girth than wit—saw fit to introduce at least a dozen of the local gentry to Charlotte as suitable partners. Naturally, those men had all rushed to sign her dance card, leaving Harrison with only one opening, and that a country dance.

Even so, he could not remember ever having enjoyed a dance as much as that. It was an allemande, and during one of the middle figures, one of the more inept of the local gallants turned to his left instead of his right and bumped squarely into Charlotte. Fortunately—or so Harrison thought—the force of the encounter was such that he was obliged to slip his arm securely around her waist to keep her from falling to the floor. As well, when she did not immediately regain her balance, he held her body against his for several seconds, offering her the support she needed.

Later, when he was obliged to relinquish her to her next partner, Harrison stood against the wall and watched her dance. The trio of two violinists and a cellist had struck up another waltz tune, and the lady was twirling gracefully down the length of the gallery, the skirt of her cherry satin gown swirling out like a bell.

Unfortunately, though she was a delight to watch, the sight of some unknown man's hand resting against the back of her waist had Harrison balling *his* hands into fists. He remembered all too well the feel of that slender waist, and he had no trouble surmising the reason for the stupid grin on her partner's loutish face.

Actually, he decided he must be losing his mind, for all he could think about were those brief moments when her body had been pressed against his. The feel of her had been a revelation. She was soft where a woman was meant to be soft, but underneath the womanly curves was a body made firm and healthy by daily activity. Until he had held Charlotte Pelham in his arms, Harrison had never suspected how alluring such a body could be. Finally, when the recollection of that experience rendered his neckcloth unbearably tight, he gave in to the inevitable and quit the room.

The instant Harrison Montgomery left the gallery, the joy went out of the evening for Charlotte. All the time she had been twirling dizzily in the waltz, smiling and pretending interest in the conversation of her partner, she had been watching Harrison standing over against the wall. She had no idea why he chose to remain at an assembly where the few females in attendance were already claimed up to the final dance; however, she enjoyed knowing he was still in the room.

As long as he was there, she could look at him whenever she wished. She could admire the broad shoulders beneath the claret-colored coat of his evening clothes . . . enjoy the contrast of his sun-bronzed

face against the pure white of his cravat. Let other
women swoon over whey-faced dandies with their
classic good looks, or make fools of themselves over
the brooding postures of poets like Lord Byron. For
Charlotte Pelham, there would never be anything to
equal the appeal of Harrison Montgomery's rugged
profile.

The Pennine Hills, sometimes called the backbone
of England, extended from the Scottish border to
about halfway down the length of England, and
straddling those rounded hills were the Yorkshire
Dales. Though nothing could rival the sumptuous
beauty of the Lake District, the ramblers found much
to admire in the Pennines, for they were offered a
choice of two worlds: the high, wild terrain of the
fells and the glorious dale bottoms with their clear,
sparkling becks and any number of charming little
gray stone villages.

The ramblers had voted unanimously to take a
more sedentary route that Tuesday morning, claiming fatigue after an evening of dancing. Charlotte
suspected, however, that their decision had less to
do with the dancing and more to do with giving
Lady Griswall an opportunity to regain her composure after yesterday's sighting of the adder.

Though the lady had declared herself quite ready
to resume the tour, and had even made a brave joke
about foolish females who made a pother over an
animal they would likely never see again, the gentlemen had formed a silent pact among themselves to
keep her in their sight the entire day, should she
become uneasy. At no time was she allowed to be
without a walking companion. And though Charlotte
had once requested that the gentlemen set aside their
chivalry and look upon the women as nothing more

than fellow travelers, she was touched by their solicitousness toward her ladyship.

The morning had gone quite well, though the walking was sometimes difficult because of tussock grass and peat bog underfoot. The area was crisscrossed by confusing gullies or groughs as the locals called them, and after a few miles, Lawrence Vinton discovered what he was certain was a bit of Roman road that bordered an isolated stretch of heathland.

Becoming quite excited at his discovery, he related to the group a story of one of the dons at Oxford. "He was walking over just such land as this, when he noticed the ground suddenly giving way under his feet."

"Oh, dear," Wilfred Bryce said. "Let us hope this ground does not give way."

"It will not," Charlotte assured them. "I have been this way many times, and the worst thing that happened to me was getting my boots all grimy." Thankfully, everyone laughed, for the last thing she needed was people fearful that they were about to disappear into some bottomless bog. "Pray tell us more, Mr. Vinton."

"According to the don," the young man continued, "when the earth fell away, it revealed a crude dwelling, which many of his learned colleagues believe could well be at least two thousand years old."

"Before the Christian era," Lady Griswall said. "How fascinating."

"Yes, ma'am."

Never very talkative, young Mr. Vinton appeared to have finished his story, and for a time no one else spoke. Apparently quite satisfied to follow what remained of the stone-paved road, the party continued walking, enjoying the quiet of the morning and the stark beauty of their surroundings. After several miles, however, they were obliged to abandon Mr.

Vinton's "Roman road" to circle around south of a peat bog. This route led them to a pastoral dale, one they all agreed was the most beautiful any rambler was likely to encounter.

The dales, which could be either gentle or wild, were formed of carboniferous limestone, which reflected the light, so on sunny days they positively gleamed. They gleamed that day when the party stopped for their midday break, beside a beck so clear its reflection might almost have been another sky.

"Oh, rare Eden," Colonel Fitzgibbon said to no one in particular.

"As usual," Wilfred Bryce replied, "you have hit the nail squarely on the head, Colonel. Eden it is. How marvelous, sir, that you always seem to know just what to say."

Letting the toadeater's remark serve for them all, no one else replied.

Even in paradise, the ground near a beck can be damp, so before she sat, Charlotte pulled her oiled cloth from her haversack and spread it out. The others, observing her actions, followed suit, and since Peter had been walking with Lady Griswall for the past mile, he asked if she cared to share his ground cover.

"Oh, no, my boy. I have my own. Besides, you may wish to stretch out for a while later. Like everyone else, you must be tired from last night's assembly."

The three younger members of the party had declined the invitation to attend the dance, but Peter did not bother to tell her ladyship that. Instead, he said, "At least allow me to spread your cloth out for you, ma'am."

"Of course. As soon as you have finished with your own. And when you return to Lancashire, I wish you will give my compliments to your mother, and tell her that her son is a gentleman any mother might be proud to . . . to . . ." Her voice did not so much trail off as the breath seemed to fall out from under it. Her hand was inside her haversack, and for a moment she did not move. Then, as if something inside her exploded, she dropped the haversack and began to scream at the top of her lungs, all the while wiping her hand across the front of her habit.

Peter, being only a foot or two from her, was the first to reach her. "Ma'am," he said, his youthful face almost as white as hers, "what is amiss?"

She did not answer; she just continued to scream and to wipe her hand across her habit, as if trying to scrub off something distasteful. Then, while Peter looked on helplessly, the lady's eyes rolled back in her head and she began to collapse. He was able to grab her by the arms before she hit the ground, thereby breaking her fall, but he was unable to lift her up. Fortunately, Harrison had come at a run, and after lifting the lady in his arms, he carried her over to the lad's cloth, where he laid her down.

By the time he had employed Peter's haversack to elevate her feet, everyone had gathered around. While the men stood about, Charlotte knelt beside the lady, who was in a complete faint. "If one of you gentlemen will wet your handkerchief in the beck," she said, "I will bathe her face and hands to see if I can revive her."

"Allow me," Wilfred Bryce said.

"Deuce take it!" the colonel all but shouted. "Do not wait for permission, man. Just do it!"

While the clerk ran to the beck, and Charlotte took her ladyship's hand and began to chaff it between her own, Harrison stepped away, taking Peter with him to a more private spot. "What happened, lad?"

"I . . . I do not know, sir. I tried to help, but I did not know what to do."

Peter's voice trembled slightly, and realizing he must still be shaken, Harrison laid his hand on the lad's shoulder, offering what comfort he might. "You did just what any man would have done, my boy. You were there, and you saved her from a nasty fall."

He gave the lad a moment to calm himself; then he tried again. "If you tell me what you saw, perhaps together we can figure out what occurred."

"Really, sir, I saw nothing out of the ordinary. Her ladyship merely reached inside her haversack for her ground cloth, and a moment later she began to scream. The rest you know."

Without another word, Harrison strode over to where Lady Griswall's haversack lay on the ground; then, lifting it carefully, he turned it upside down and dumped the contents onto the ground. Out fell her packet of sandwiches, her flask of tea, and the shallow drinking bowl, the ground cover, and an adder. As the snake hit the ground, Harrison did not even bother to step back. There was no need, for the reptile was quite dead; it had been for at least twenty-four hours. His head had been completely severed hours before, and only the body remained.

"What I do not understand," Charlotte said later that evening, when all but Lady Griswall were gathered around the dinner table, "is how the reptile got in her haversack? And why?"

"With a severed head," Jonathan said, anger making him speak sharply, "it certainly did not crawl in there!"

The colonel cleared his throat. "A cruel joke surely."

"Joke or not," Andrew Vinton said, shaking his fist, "if I catch the bas—the person who put it there, I will give him something he will not long forget."

"Whoever he may be," Russell Throne added, looking about at the faces of his fellow travelers, "he has a deuced warped sense of what is amusing."

"Perhaps," the colonel continued, "we would be better not knowing the identity of the culprit. 'When ignorance is bliss,' don't you know, ' 'tis folly to be wise.' "

In this instance, Charlotte was more inclined to side with Mr. Vinton's philosophy than the poet's. "When Thomas Gray penned his *Ode on a Distant Prospect of Eton College*, I cannot think he meant we should remain ignorant of the identity of the perpetrator of such a malicious act. To do such a thing is unthinkable. And, I might add, unpardonable."

She breathed deeply, as if to control her temper; then, in a calmer, though no less passionate voice, she added, "I pray the Heavenly Father will forgive this cruelty, for I vow I will not."

Charlotte spent the better part of the night sitting beside Lady Griswall's bed, assuring her from time to time that there were no creatures crawling beneath the covers or lurking behind the nightstand. Just before dawn, when the lady still had not slept, Charlotte accepted the landlord's offer to have his "rib" prepare a tisane laced with laudanum. Once the tisane was drunk, and her ladyship had fallen asleep, Charlotte left her in the capable hands of her maid.

Knowing she would never sleep now, and feeling the need for a breath of fresh air, Charlotte went to her bedchamber, changed from her dinner dress into one of her habits and her boots, and let herself out the front entrance of the small inn. She did not walk far, merely to the edge of the inn yard, to a wide oak tree that had been recently pollarded. Seating herself on the forest "stool," she gazed up at the sky that had already begun to change from black to morning gray.

"Are you all right, Miss Pelham?"

Charlotte recognized the voice as belonging to Harrison Montgomery, and though it was unusual for any of the party to be awake at this hour, she did not ask him why he was there. Instead, she did what she had been wanting to do for the past sixteen hours; she put her face in her hands and wept.

For just an instant, Harrison was too surprised to move, though why it should be so, he could not say. If anyone had the right to a good cry, that person was Charlotte Pelham, and before he quite realized what he was doing, he sat beside her on the pollarded oak and put his arm around her shoulder.

As if she had been doing so all her life, she turned toward him and hid her face in his shoulder, giving vent to tears so copious they soon soaked right through his coat, his waistcoat, and his shirt. Not that Harrison minded. Obeying man's primitive instinct to protect the female of the species, he wrapped both arms around her and held her tight, letting her cry until there were no tears left, only an occasional snuffle.

"Here," he said, offering her his handkerchief. "If I know anything of the matter, a cry that good deserves an equally good blow." He had hoped she would laugh; instead she moved as if to pull out of his arms. "Do not," he said, tightening his embrace.

"But I am ruining your coat."

"I have others."

"That is as may be, but I should not be crying on your shoulder. And," she added, trying once again to move away, "you should not be holding me."

"Perhaps not," he said, not giving an inch, "but I am bigger than you, and stronger than you, and for once you are going to let someone else take charge."

"But I am all better now, I assure you."

"I do not doubt it. No more than I doubt your courage or your ability to cope with whatever challenge comes your way. Just this once, however, I think it permissible for you to let down your guard a little. Word of a gentleman, I will not tell."

"Gentleman, indeed," she said, taking the proffered handkerchief and blowing her nose in a most ungenteel fashion. Once she had finished with the handkerchief, she returned her head to his shoulder, this time resting her cheek against his damp lapel. "Do not think I have forgotten that you blackmailed me into allowing you to join this group."

"Nor should you forget, for as the colonel would say, "Once a blackmailer, always a blackmailer.' "

"I think the expression is 'Once a thief.' "

"Thief? Really?"

She nodded. When she returned her head to his chest, her clean, sweet-smelling hair brushed against his lips, adding yet another delightful sensation to the pleasure he felt holding her in his arms.

"If I have misquoted, then forget I said anything, for I am most certainly not a thief. Not unless purloining a peach from my neighbor's succession house counts."

She chuckled. "Did you purloin your neighbor's peaches?"

"Peach singular," he said. "I was about fourteen at the time, and I stole the fruit for one of the milkmaids. She wanted to taste a peach, yet she was afraid she would be fired if she were caught taking it."

"Then you were just being kind."

"Not a bit of it."

"But—"

"As I said, I was fourteen, and the milkmaid was the prettiest girl I had ever seen. Once she had eaten the stolen peach, I took my reward by stealing a kiss from her lips."

Charlotte's breath caught in her throat, for once his story was told, he put a finger beneath her chin and lifted her face. "Just like this," he said; then he bent his head and brushed his lips gently against hers.

Charlotte had never before felt anything so sweet, so tender, and she remained perfectly still, afraid to move and break the magic spell of his kiss. When he lifted his head, it was all she could do not to wrap her arms around his neck and beg for another taste. She might have done so, too, if she had not heard the sound of boots crunching on the gravel of the inn yard.

Without a word, he dropped his arms from around her, leaving her feeling unbelievably cold; then he stood and walked back to the inn. He did not look back, and when he passed whoever had been walking in the inn yard, he muttered a greeting, then continued toward the door of the inn.

Charlotte touched her fingers to her lips, hoping to keep the warmth of his kiss there for just a moment longer. Sadly, it did not work. The kiss was gone, just like the man who had given it to her.

She sat there on the pollarded oak for a long time, until the gray sky was streaked with pink, all the while reliving what had happened to her. Harrison Montgomery had said he was not a thief, but Charlotte knew differently. She was very much afraid he had just stolen her heart.

Chapter Eleven

When Peter drove the luggage wagon from the inn yard that Wednesday morning, Benizur did not follow in the Tilbury. Instead, the turbaned little man remained behind to drive Lady Griswall and her maid to the nearest village so they could catch the afternoon stage headed south to Harrogate.

Charlotte had understood perfectly why her ladyship did not wish to continue the tour; she understood, and she did not blame her in the least. Still, the lady felt she was deserting Charlotte. "But, my dear child, you will now be without a chaperone. And do not bother reminding me that your brother is present, for you and I both know that a young man, no matter how devoted he may be to his sister's welfare, is not a suitable substitute for an older or a married female. Especially when the sister is traveling in company with six other gentlemen who are in no way related to her."

The truth of the observation was undeniable, but Charlotte could not turn back now. There were five more days to be got through, and proper chaperonage was the least of her worries. There were now only six paying ramblers left, and if one more should drop out before they reached Robin Hood's Bay, Charlotte would forfeit not only any hope of future employment, but her pay for this tour as well.

After bidding the tearful Lady Griswall farewell,

Charlotte joined the group, who waited for her outside the small inn. She did not put the day's route to a vote; instead, she told them they would be traveling over the fells for the day. Fortunately, no one objected, for she was in need of some real activity—activity so strenuous it would put all else from her mind.

The route required walking mixed with an occasional bit of actual climbing, and for the entire morning Charlotte moved at her own pace, not caring how far ahead she got. She finally stopped when the fell dropped away abruptly in a steep, north-facing escarpment, an escarpment that offered a sudden, very impressive view of the distant Yorkshire moors. Even in her present troubled state, she was struck by the vastness of the open, unobstructed space.

Enjoying a quietness interrupted only by the loud, clear whistle of a curlew circling overhead, and delighting in the feeling of oneness with nature that mountaintops always provided, she sat on the edge of the escarpment, dangling her feet over the side in a manner she would have forbidden one of the other tour members. She had been sitting there for several minutes, trying to free her mind of her troubles, when Harrison Montgomery came around the turn in the track and stopped, struck as she had been by the magnificent view. Somehow, she was not surprised that he was the first of the ramblers to catch up with her.

"How far can one see?" he asked.

"It appears to go on forever, but the actual distance might be anywhere from twenty to forty miles."

He did not join her, but remained on the narrow track, some four feet away. Quietly, he said, "Considering what happened to Mrs. Richardson at the gorge, I wonder if it is altogether wise for you to sit so close to the edge."

"I know what I am doing." The reply came out

sharper than Charlotte had intended, but at the moment she was in no frame of mind to offer an apology.

"Do you?" he asked.

She nodded. "I have done this many times. Though until this moment, it was mine and my father's little secret."

With her hands on the ground beside her, she leaned forward, observing her dangling feet almost as if they belonged to someone else. "When I was a little girl, any time my father and I climbed a mountain, we would sit like this once we reached the summit. It was our reward for expending the energy required. 'Sitting on top of the world,' Father used to call it. Only I was not supposed to tell my mother."

"Mrs. Pelham would have disapproved?"

"Mrs. Williams, now. And, yes, she would have disapproved. Vehemently. Of me, of the things I loved to do, of my father's influence on me, all of it. Mother insisted that if Father continued to indulge me in my love of outdoor activities, I would never grow into a proper young lady." She shrugged. "Oh, well. I suppose she was correct."

Harrison did not know how to respond to the remark, so he chose the better part of valor. His decision must have been the right one, for after a few moments of silence, she continued. "Mother was always fearful that some catastrophe would happen to one or both of us, and that is why we never told her we climbed mountains. Had she known, she would have insisted my father stop taking me with him on his walks. Because of her fear, Father would have had to travel alone, and I would have been obliged to remain at home like a proper young lady, stitching samplers."

"And you would have hated that."

"I would have loathed it. And loathed myself as well. Lancashire is full of sampler sewers. Why should

I add to their ranks, when I could be sitting on top of the world?"

For the life of him, Harrison could not think of a single reason why she should give up what she loved doing simply to satisfy someone else's idea of what was proper, or to ease someone else's fears. Except, of course, *his* fear for her.

"Has it occurred to you?" he asked at last, "that females have been the object of both the mishaps on this trip? And that you are now the only female left?"

"Has it occurred to you," she countered, "that I am not a fool?"

"Many times. Until," he added, "I saw you sitting on top of the world."

With a sigh of resignation, she swung her feet back onto solid ground and stood. "Satisfied?" she asked.

"Almost."

"Almost? What more must I do to please you? That is, assuming I *wished* to please you."

"I will assume only that you wish to avoid any further mishaps."

She took one last look at the glorious view; then she joined him on the path. "I am willing to listen to any suggestions that would minimize the chance of further unpleasantness."

Harrison did not tell her what Dora Richardson had told him the morning after her accident—that she did not fall, but was nudged from behind—for the young woman had been unable to offer any real proof of her suspicions. Though Harrison was inclined to believe she was in the right of it, he had no desire to ruin some innocent man's reputation without solid evidence. Still, if she was correct, then there was the matter of Charlotte's safety to be considered. "There is something I wish you to think about."

"Yes?"

"Excluding your brothers, there are six men in this

group. Unfortunately, one of those six men is at best a coward and at worst a monster."

"And you suspect this coward-monster may have plans for me?"

"I do. And for that reason, I propose that either Jonathan, Peter, or I remain close to you at all times."

"An interesting proposal, and I would agree without reservation, except for one thing."

"And that is?"

"You, sir, are one of the six men."

Before he could reply to her observation, Harrison heard the sound of voices, and within moments the Vinton brothers appeared around the track.

"I say!" Lawrence Vinton observed, stopping suddenly. "What a magnificent sight."

"Rather!" his older brother agreed. Andrew walked to the spot where Charlotte had sat earlier and looked his fill of the panoramic view. "I vow it makes one feel as if the rest of the world is very far away, and that one has found privacy at last. Do you not agree, Miss Pelham?"

"Perfectly," she replied.

Harrison paid no attention to the solicitor's banter; all he could think of was that Charlotte numbered *him* among the suspects. Not that he could blame her. After all, he suspected each of the other five, including the two who stood before him at the moment. Lawrence was still young enough to think putting a dead snake in someone's haversack a capital jest; however, Harrison could not envision the lad intentionally nudging a young woman standing at the edge of a precipice.

As for the older Mr. Vinton, it was difficult for Harrison to judge him with anything like fairness. The handsome solicitor went out of his way to make himself agreeable to Charlotte, and as a consequence, he made himself objectionable to Harrison.

If he ruled out the Vintons as suspects, it left only the windbag, the clerk, and the birder. Of those three, Colonel Fitzgibbon and Wilfred Bryce were the least likely candidates, for they had not had access to the snake. Russell Thorne had been in charge of watching the reptile, and as far as Harrison could determine, he was the last one to leave the area.

Furthermore, it was quite possible that Thorne had been offended by her ladyship's having laughed at him over the matter of the mouse stealing his stocking. Some males did not take well to being laughed at by females. And if Thorne was angry, then Harrison would be doubly watchful of Charlotte, for she had laughed too. Of course, Harrison had laughed as well, but smaller men did not generally provoke males they knew to be both taller and stronger.

Damnation! What a revolting task, trying to determine which of one's fellow travelers was scoundrel enough to assuage his frustrations by terrorizing females. Revolting or not, it was imperative that Harrison determine which man was guilty.

Deuce take it! He had come on this cursed tour to discover if either Jonathan or Peter was the brother he lost more than a dozen years ago, and at the moment he was no closer to solving that riddle than he had been the first day out of St. Bee's Head. Twelve years! And yet he was proposing to forsake his own investigation in order to protect a female he had not known existed until little more than a week ago. Which just proved what fools men could be!

Fool or not, Harrison made a point that evening of having a private talk with Jonathan and Peter. The inn where they stopped for the night was quite remote, and not up to their usual standards; even counting the ramblers, there were fewer than a dozen guests. Naturally, after having lost one more of their party, and having had the most strenuous day of walking so far, they were all too tired to do more than eat their dinner, then go immediately to their rooms.

Charlotte was, of course, the first to leave the rather threadbare private parlor, and while she bid everyone a good evening, Harrison whispered to Jonathan that he wished to speak with him and Peter. Scarcely quarter of an hour later, when the three of them were alone, standing at a window heavily draped with moth-eaten red velvet hangings, Harrison wasted no time in explaining his plan.

"This morning I mentioned to Miss Pelham that I think she would be wise not to go anyplace without one of the three of us in attendance. Just, you understand, until the end of this trip."

"And her reply?" Jonathan asked.

Harrison smiled. "At least she did not throw anything at me."

At that, both lads laughed. "Consider yourself fortunate," Jonathan said.

"Unquestionably," Peter concurred.

Almost instantly, they were both somber again, with Jonathan speaking first. "Peter and I were talking about this very subject last night, after the incident with the snake in her ladyship's haversack. And Peter thinks— Well, you tell him, Peter."

The other lad cleared his throat as if embarrassed. "If you remember, sir, I was one of the people nearest Mrs. Richardson when she went over the side of the gorge."

Harrison remembered quite well, for Peter and Andrew Vinton were holding the lady, keeping her from falling farther, when he had reached across to pull her the final few feet to safety. "Had it not been for your quick action, lad, the lady might well have fallen to her death."

The young man lowered his gaze, obviously embarrassed to be singled out for such praise. "Anyone would have done the same."

"Perhaps," Harrison said. "In any event, I do not believe you brought up the subject to garner laurel wreaths."

"Good Lord, no!"

"Tell him," Jonathan said.

Peter lifted the badly frayed cord of the window drapery nearest him, studying it rather than looking at Harrison. "I hope, sir, that you will not think me foolish, for I have no proof, but I do not believe Mrs. Richardson fell."

"Nor does she."

"What!" both young men said at once.

"The lady told me she was nudged from behind. By accident or design, she could not say. Personally, I have begun to suspect it was by design."

"By Jove! You were right, Peter."

In his relief at being believed, the young man stepped back, completely forgetting he still held the frayed drapery cord. With but the slightest tug, the entire drapery fell down, wooden rod and all, and when the considerable dust settled, Jonathan was coughing, and Peter was rubbing the back of his head.

"Are you hurt, lad?"

"Nothing to signify, sir. The rod merely grazed me."

"Here. Let me have a look. In case you need a court plaster."

Never one to look a gift horse in the mouth, Harrison did not wait for permission; he merely examined the boy's head, paying special attention to that area behind the left ear. Unfortunately, if there had ever been an injury there, it had left no scar.

More disappointed than he would have thought possible, he reminded himself that there was still one other lad to examine. "Come," he said. "Let us make plans as to who will watch Charlotte at what time. Do you drive the wagon tomorrow, Jonathan?"

"Yes, sir."

"Then I suggest you take the morning watch, Peter, and I will take over after the midday break."

Charlotte lay in the narrow, lumpy bed for some time, gazing at the raftered ceiling of the tiny, upper-floor bedchamber, unable to fall asleep. Her body was willing, especially after the grueling pace she had set today, but her mind would not cooperate. All manner of questions raced through her brain, pursuing ever-illusive answers. Harrison Montgomery had not been the first to plant seeds of doubt as to her safety, and during the first part of the morning's climb, she had finally admitted to herself that too many accidents had happened on this walk.

Not that mishaps were anything new when one went on a long-distance ramble. Over the years, she and her father had experienced a number of misadventures. Those mishaps, however, usually came in the form of blisters on the heels and toes, uprooted trees that blocked the narrow mountain paths, or punts that overturned, dumping the paddlers into icy waters. Once, when they camped out, she had awakened during the night to find a little spiny hedgehog nibbling at the toe of her boot. Still, in several years of travels, nothing truly frightening had ever happened.

After reviewing the present situation, three questions reigned supreme. Were the recent events truly accidents? If not, then who had orchestrated them? And lastly, why had he done so?

There was one more question that bothered Charlotte even more than the other three, and she hoped

with all her heart that the answer to that question
was "No." Could the perpetrator of this trip's misfor-
tunes be Harrison Montgomery?

If she looked at the situation dispassionately—
without remembering that soft, gentle kiss, and without
recalling the way her heart threatened to stop every
time he came near—Harrison was the likeliest candi-
date, for he was the only member of the group who
had ever given her a moment's trouble.

His very appearance at St. Bee's Head had been
mysterious—a wealthy nabob and that odd little turbaned man who was not a servant, but who did not
join them for meals. Firstly, Harrison had come to the
group late and unannounced, and he was completely
unprepared for a cross-country walk. Secondly, he
had practically forced Charlotte to allow him to join
the tour, without offering the least explanation for
his wish to travel with them. And finally, although
he had been reasonably subtle about it, she had noticed that he had taken an interest in both Peter and
Jonathan, asking them all manner of questions about
their lives at school and in Lancashire.

Why should he do that? Why would a man of the
world, a man who, according to Lady Griswall, had
set the *ton* on its ear, be interested in the lives of two
boys not yet up at university? Charlotte loved Peter
and Jonathan, but even allowing for her partiality,
she did not feel they had that much of interest to
relate.

It was all most troubling, and the more she sought
answers, the more the number of questions grew.
The last thing she remembered before sleep finally
claimed her was a prayer whispered in the darkness.
"Please," she begged, "do not let the monster be
Harrison."

Chapter Twelve

Thursday morning, the eleventh day of the tour, just before leaving the shabby little inn, the ramblers voted to keep to the low trails that day. The first few hours of the day they would see the last of Pennines, and later they would begin their trek across the beginnings of the North York Moors. Moorlands, like heaths, are usually desolate areas where dying vegetation accumulates and eventually becomes peat, with the major difference between heath and moor being that the more abundant rainfall on the moors makes them boggy and marshy.

Naturally, walking is slower on the damp, springy earth, so once they finished their midday meal, Charlotte led the party on a circuitous, yet much more scenic route down into the last of the dales. After the starkness of the moorland, the dale—dotted with the remaining oak, elm, and yew trees not hacked down by the inhabitants of the previous century—was a welcome sight.

The ramblers followed an ancient track, the type the panniersmen of old called a trod, and while they traveled, Harrison kept a watchful eye on Charlotte. If she appreciated his efforts, however, she gave no indication of it. In fact, any attempt on his part to engage her in conversation was treated on her part with cool detachment, and though she never gave him the cut direct, any questions from him received answers so brief they bordered on the impolite.

He bore up under this treatment well enough, until Russell Thorne approached Charlotte and engaged her in conversation. Their exchange was so liberally laced with pleasant-sounding chitchat, not to mention the occasional chuckle, that Harrison ground his teeth in frustration. *How dare she be gracious to that bird-watcher, yet give me the cold shoulder.*

"And that one," Thorne said, calling her attention to a gray-breasted bird with an orange-and-yellow beak, "is a moorhen. I gave her part of my bread earlier, and now she is trailing after me in hopes of further largesse."

"How clever of her," Charlotte said. "And of you!"

Clever indeed! One would think the man invented the bird, instead of merely enticing it with a few scraps.

Harrison waited only until Thorne had dropped back to bore the colonel with his incessant chatter about bird life; then he approached Charlotte again. "So," he began, not bothering to temper his voice, "for others you have a smile and a kind word, ever trusting that they mean you no harm. And all the while you treat me like a pariah."

"I was not aware," she said, "that I was treating you any differently from the other members of the party."

"You are, and you know it."

"I know nothing of the sort. The colonel, Mr. Bryce, Andrew Vinton. You are all entitled to the same measure of my time."

"Andrew? You call Vinton by his name? How cozy. I wonder what you will call him if he should prove to be the one responsible for driving the Richardsons and Lady Griswall from the group?"

Her eyes flashed with anger. "And if it does *not*

prove to be him? In truth, it might just as easily be any one of you."

When Harrison had gotten out of bed that morning, his only intention had been to protect Charlotte Pelham. Now, here he was arguing with her, a circumstance that could prompt her to do something foolish in order to avoid his company. The thought had no more than occurred to him when she did something exceedingly foolish.

Obviously she was too angry with him to remember one of the basic rules of safety, for when she came to a fallen tree, she did not tap it as she should to test for hidden animals before stepping over it. Instead, she stepped directly on top of the log. Too late she realized her mistake. The log had lain there for so long it was rotted through, and the moment she put her entire weight on it, the wood gave way and both her feet sank inside the limb.

Immediately, Harrison heard a slight buzz that grew far too quickly into a frenzied protest.

"Heaven help us!" he muttered.

Reacting to the growing noise, he grabbed Charlotte around her waist and lifted her out of the log. As he had suspected, her boots were covered with honey. Seconds after he pulled her away from the destroyed hive, bees began to appear, furious with whomever was responsible for the unwarranted invasion of their ordered lives.

Without waiting to discuss the matter, Harrison snatched her hand and yelled, "Run!"

Charlotte did not need further encouragement. Obeying what seemed the most sensible advice she had received in a decade, she ran. The bees were in no mood to be forgiving, and when Charlotte fled, leaving a trail of honey, they gave chase. Her hat fell off at some point, and she felt several of the angry insects diving at her hair.

Hoping not to bring the wrath of the bees down on the rest of the party, she and Harrison did not run the way the had just come; instead, they bore off to their left, in the direction of a small beck. With the irate swarm gaining on them by the second, neither of them hesitated. As if they were of one mind, they both leaped down the four or five feet from the bank; then, after drawing a deep breath, they threw themselves face first into the shallow water.

Charlotte could not tell how long they remained submerged in the icy beck; at the time it felt like hours. When she could hold her breath no longer, and was forced to decide between death by bee venom or death by suffocation, she flipped onto her back and lifted her nose just above the water level. Fortunately, nothing attacked her nose, and as she inhaled gratefully, Harrison broke through the water, gasping for air.

Once he sat up, he caught her by the shoulders and sat her up as well. For both their sakes, it was fortunate the majority of the bees had flown past them, hopefully abandoning their vendetta; otherwise, they could have been subjected to multiple stings. As it was, Charlotte felt a slight burning in the side of her neck, just beneath her sodden neckcloth, and as she pulled at the lace jabot that was tied in a single knot, Harrison took the matter out of her hands and ripped the material in two.

"Are you stung?" he asked.

"A fine thing if I were not, after you turned my best lace into a cleaning rag."

Her sarcasm made no impression on him, for he was too busy running his hands inside her neckcloth, searching for bees. Fortunately, he found only one, and that one, having already used its stinger, was dead.

Dozens more dead bees floated on top of the water,

and Harrison dropped the one he found beside the others. Charlotte remained perfectly still, sitting in the shallow stream, and allowed Harrison to search for the stinger.

"I have it," he said. "Do not move."

Reaching inside his seaman's jacket, he removed a long, thin dagger—a rather dangerous-looking possession for a man supposedly out for a carefree ramble—and using the sharp point, he flicked the stinger out of her skin.

"Here," he said, when she cupped her hand and pressed icy water at the spot. "Let me."

Without waiting for permission, he cupped his much larger hand, scooped up an ounce or two of water, then put his hand back inside her neckcloth, allowing the cold water to trickle slowly onto her skin.

"I assure you, Mr. Montgomery, that is not at all necessary."

"Just this once," he said, "humor me."

Scooping up more water, he put his hand inside her neckcloth again, and this time, when the water had all trickled out, he flattened his cool palm against her neck, holding it gently, his strong fingers cupped around her nape. To Charlotte's embarrassment, she experienced an unexpected giddy feeling—a giddiness that had nothing to do with the bee sting. It was the feel of his large, competent hand against her skin that made her heart race and her breathing accelerate.

She willed herself not to react to his touch, but when she looked up at him, he was watching her, and his gray eyes had taken on a smokey quality. Something about that look increased her giddiness, and she reached up and caught his wrist, giving it a light tug to pull his hand away. He did not allow it.

"I . . . I am fine," she said, her voice surprisingly hoarse. "You may let me go."

"And if I do not wish to let you go?"

Harrison knew exactly what was making her sound hoarse; she was reacting to his touch. And after the cold shoulder she had shown him earlier, it pleased him to know he was making her uncomfortable. When she lowered her eyelids so he could not read her thoughts, he slowly, yet deliberately slipped his other hand inside her neckcloth as well, and while he held her slender neck between his palms, he used his thumbs to ease up her chin. "Shall I kiss it and make it better?"

Unsure if he meant her lips or her neck, Charlotte said nothing. Apparently, he took her silence for acquiescence, for he lowered his head. Just before their lips touched, however, she heard the sound of running feet.

"Miss Pelham," Wilfred Bryce said, "are you injured?"

"Merely a bee sting, Mr. Bryce."

"If you will allow it, ma'am, I will be happy to see if I can help. Not that I know that much about bees, you understand. My ignorance notwithstanding, you see me ready and willing to do all within my humble power to be of assistance."

"And you call *me* a blackmailer," Harrison whispered. "There is nothing more difficult to refuse than help or advice from a person who cloaks himself in humility—be it real or imagined."

Charlotte agreed wholeheartedly. In fact, she would love to tell Wilfred Bryce to take his humbleness and his ineptness away, for he had ruined what had promised to be a lovely moment. Instead, she said, "Thank you, sir, but Mr. Montgomery was good enough to locate the stinger and remove it. Now, if he will help me to stand, I will ask you to give me a hand up the bank.''

With an audience watching their every move, Harrison had no recourse but to do as she asked, so he stood and helped her to her feet. Her boots were filled with water, and her habit, which was completely waterlogged, clung to her from her thighs to ankles, making walking almost impossible. Obviously thinking only to facilitate their exit from the beck, Harrison swept her up into his arms and carried her the few feet to the bank, where Wilfred Bryce stood waiting.

Charlotte had very little faith in the clumsy clerk's ability to assist her; however, she had said he might give her a hand up the bank, and she could not spurn his help now. Feeling far from confident, she closed her eyes while Harrison placed her in Bryce's waiting arms, not at all certain she would not wind up back in the water. To her surprise, Bryce lifted her with ease, and when he made his way back up the bank, his footing was sure and his movements confident.

Charlotte had placed her arms around his shoulders, and she could feel the rock-hard muscles in his back and upper arms bunching. No one could have been more amazed than she; it seemed that the bumbling clerk had improved out of all proportion during the past week.

When Charlotte awoke the next morning, she lay in the cramped little bedchamber of the next-to-the-last inn on their schedule of stops. Closing her ears to the sounds of people stirring below stairs, she tried to recall the feeling she had experienced yesterday in the beck, when Harrison had tilted her face upward. ''Shall I kiss it and make it better?'' he had asked. Though her lips had remained still, her heart had yelled, "Yes! Yes! Kiss me, by all means."

And he would have kissed her, had Wilfred Bryce not arrived at just the wrong moment. Not that she was too surprised by that, for if there was a wrong place to be, Wilfred Bryce would be there. Similarly, if there was an error to be made, he would make it.

That last prophecy was fulfilled that very afternoon, when Bryce was walking near Jonathan and Lawrence Vinton. One minute everything was perfectly normal; then, somehow, the clerk lost his footing. In his attempt to break his fall, Bryce kicked Jonathan rather hard in the left shin, and he, too, went down.

How the clerk managed to trip was a mystery, for the ground undulated gently, and the turf was springy. In late summer the area would burst into bloom, with purple heather stretching as far as the eye could see. With the heather in bloom, a person might easily step into an unseen rabbit hole and fall. But in late May, there was little more than the occasional bit of bracken and a few bog plants—nothing to cause a man with reasonably good eyesight to trip.

Jonathan was not a complainer, but from the way he bit his lower lip when Harrison and Mr. Thorne helped him to stand, it was obvious the blow to his shin had been quite painful. Thankfully, the bone did not appear to be broken. Still, the group was obliged to wait for a time while Charlotte bound the lad's shin in a snug bandage.

Even with the aid of the bandage, Jonathan had difficulty keeping pace with the other ramblers, and since they were scheduled to sleep beneath the stars that evening, they decided to stop early. They set up their campsite within sight of an abandoned hot spring, where the soldiers of Hadrian's Legions had once built a Roman bath, with the gentlemen leaving their bedrolls and haversacks on one side of the clearing containing the few remaining ruins and Charlotte leaving her things on the other side.

Once they were settled in, Harrison suggested to Charlotte that he and Andrew Vinton help Jonathan walk the three miles to the inn where Peter had taken the wagon for the night. "The lad can lean on us," he said. "Use us like a pair of crutches."

Charlotte was more grateful than she could say for the suggestion and for the thoughtfulness. "Thank you so much. I did not like thinking about Jonathan having to suffer through tomorrow's walk."

"Then it is settled. Once we escort your brother to the inn, where he can rest, I will ask Benizur to see to the lad's comfort. Or would you prefer that we leave Peter to look after him?"

"Bring Peter back," she said, "and thank Benizur for me. I am persuaded my brother will do well enough driving the wagon tomorrow to the final inn, and unless I miss my guess, Peter will be more than happy to sleep out-of-doors."

"You cannot know how sorry I am," Bryce said, delaying their departure so he might apologize for perhaps the sixth time. "I hope you will not hold it against me, Mr. Pelham. And, of course, if there is anything I can do to relieve your suffering, I pray you will not hesitate to apprise me of it."

"You can stop talking," Harrison told the clerk none too politely, "and let us be on our way."

"Of course. Of course. A thousand pardons. I assure you, I had no desire to add to the young gentleman's distress. And if you will forgive me—and you, too, of course, Mr. Vinton—I promise to be more considerate in the future. I realize I do run on a bit sometimes, but—"

The gentlemen did not hear the remainder of his apology, for they merely turned and walked away. Unlike the men, Charlotte could not escape, and the clerk remained by her side for the next half hour. "I really am sorry," he said.

"You have made that abundantly clear, Mr. Bryce, and I beg you will not mention the matter again. Now, if you will excuse—"

"Poor Miss Pelham. So many problems besetting you. Forgive my curiosity, ma'am, but are there usually so many mishaps on a tour of this kind? Being a novice myself, I did not know."

Charlotte wanted to scream at the man to go away and leave her in peace. She needed to be alone. With this latest accident, she was beginning to feel as vulnerable as Damocles seated beneath the sword that hung from a single hair. After this night there were but two more to be got through, and she was almost afraid to see what those two nights would bring. As eager as she had been to begin this cross-country walk, she was now far more eager to see it come to an end.

For now, though, all she wanted was to eat her dinner in solitude. Later, she had every intention of trying out the hot spring and discovering for herself what made the Romans build so many baths. She could not do that, however, until everyone else was asleep, and she had some much-needed privacy. Of course, she could say none of that to Wilfred Bryce. He was a paying member of the tour, and as such, she could not be rude to him, no matter the provocation.

"To answer your question, Mr. Bryce, we do seem to have been remarkably unfortunate on this trip."

"Unfortunate? I wonder."

A shiver ran up Charlotte's spine. "Whatever do you mean?"

"Nothing, I assure you. Only . . ."

"Only what?"

"Only this, Miss Pelham. If it were not such a pre-posterous idea, I would think that someone was de-liberately trying to keep you from finishing the tour."

Again that frisson of uncertainty traveled up her spine. "And why would someone want to do that?"

"I am sure I do not know. After all, I am merely a clerk. I do what I am told and I mind my own business. However, if I were to hazard a guess as to why anyone would want the tour to end prema-turely, my guess would be to prove that you could not do the job."

Night had fallen, and the moon had risen in all its fullness when Harrison returned to the Roman ruins. "Thank you, sir," Peter said, "for bringing Jonathan to the inn and for accompanying me back to the campsite."

"Think nothing of it, lad."

The two of them were alone, for Mr. Andrew Vin-ton had decided to remain at the inn. While they waited in the taproom for Peter to get his bedroll, the solicitor's eye had been caught by a promising-looking barmaid with blond braids and a generous bosom, and nothing would do him but to put his luck to the test.

Just before they reached the ruins of the Roman bath, Harrison decided to put *his* luck to the test as well, by asking the question he had been wanting to ask for the past twelve days. "Forgive my bluntness, Peter, but there is something I must know. Believe me, your answer is more important to me than I can say. Otherwise I would not intrude upon your privacy."

"You may ask me anything, sir."

Now that the time had come, Harrison had trouble giving voice to the most important question. Instead, he decided to work his way up to it. "Are you, in fact, related by blood to the Pelhams?"

The lad hesitated a moment; then he said, "No, sir. We are not related by blood, though I feel as close to them as if I were their brother."

Harrison took a deep breath and expelled it before braving the next question. "And do you have a brother of your own?"

The young man shook his head.

"You are certain?"

"Yes, sir. Quite certain. I am an only child, though I always wished I'd had a big brother."

That last statement made it difficult for Harrison to swallow. "You are, are you not, Peter Newsome, Squire Newsome's adopted son?"

"Adopted?"

"Yes. At age four."

"I am Peter Newsome, and the squire is, indeed, my father. My *real* father. I am not adopted."

Harrison was quiet for some time. He could not believe how despondent the lad's answer left him. "Not adopted?" he said at last.

"No, sir."

"Are you sure? Sometimes parents do not tell a child, because they fear he will one day want to seek his real family."

"The Newsomes *are* my real family. I am not adopted."

Not ready to admit defeat, Harrison said, "Does the name Timothy James mean anything to you?"

"No, sir, it does not. Should it?"

"What about Anne or Thomas James?"

"No, sir."

Desperation made Harrison grab at straws. Perhaps the lad would remember their old nurse, who loved them more dearly than their own mother. "What of Nanny Clark? Surely you remember her."

"I am sorry, Mr. Montgomery, but I do not know any of those people. Should I?"

"Only if you are Timmy James."

"Which I am not. As I told you, I am Peter Newsome. I have always been Peter Newsome."

Something like a lead weight seemed to press down on Harrison's lungs, making it difficult for him to breathe. He had been so hopeful. Deep inside him, where there remained the one last shred of faith that a very hard life had not been able to take from him, he had believed that one of the lads was Timmy. He had thought that if he could only determine which one of them was Charlotte's brother, the other would automatically be his.

"I am sorry," Peter said.

"So am I, lad. More sorry than I can say."

Chapter Thirteen

Harrison did not return to the men's side of the Roman ruin to claim his bedroll. What was the point? He knew he would not sleep. Not yet. Not while he felt as if he had been attacked by a Bengal tiger and left torn and bleeding, with no one to bind up his wounds.

He had not found Timmy. And worse yet, he feared he might never find him.

The squire and his lady had been his best lead so far, for the clerk from Chancery Court had sworn he remembered the case. "Newsomes from Lancashire," he had said. Bow Street had traced the name to the village of Burley, and Harrison had let his burning need to find his little brother convince him that he had the right family.

Now, it was all to do over again. The endless search. The leads that went nowhere. The people willing to be *anyone's* relative if the price was right. And with each new search, the resulting disappointments.

With the paper trail lost or misplaced somewhere in the centuries' worth of files in Chancery Court, where was Harrison to start this time? He might as well stop every fifteen-year-old boy in England to ask him if his name had ever been Timmy.

Even if by some stroke of luck Harrison should approach the right fifteen-year-old, there was no guarantee the boy would remember what had happened when he was four years old. Did a person remember that far back? Harrison was not sure *he* remembered anything from that age. Of course, he had not been taken from his home and all he knew at that tender age, so his childhood memories were all of the same people and the same place. For him, one year's memories had pretty much blended with another.

Timmy, Timmy, Timmy. Where are you, little brother? I thought if only I had enough money I could find you. Sadly, I was wrong. And if I do not find you, of what good is all my money?

While these unproductive thoughts chased one another through his head, Harrison walked aimlessly, uncaring where he went. He might have continued walking for some time had the toe of his boot not collided with something hard and unforgiving. "Damnation!" he muttered, looking to see what he had stumbled across.

When he bent to look more closely, the light from the full moon revealed what he decided must be a section of one of the interior walls of the Roman bath. This insignificant reminder of what had once been the greatest army in the world, was no more than a remnant some eight or ten inches high, with most of the wall's baked tiles now broken. Interested in spite of his previous disappointment, Harrison followed the wall some fifty feet or more before it disappeared entirely.

Not ten feet beyond the vanishing point, however, he spied six steps, which might have been carved of marble. The sides of each step were encrusted with moss, while the tops, worn smooth by the soles of who-knew-how-many pairs of sandal-covered feet, gleamed white in the bright glow of the full moon.

Moving carefully, Harrison placed his foot on the

first slab. When it did not quiver beneath his weight, he took the second step, then the third, slowly descending into some sort of rectangular, subterranean chamber. There was no roof, of course, or he would not have continued, not with only the moonlight to guide his way.

This had to be the bath itself, for unless Harrison mistook the matter, he heard flowing water close by. There was a second wall just in front of him, or at least a section of a wall, and this one, too, was tiled and cool to the touch. It was about five feet high and four feet long, and not two feet to his left was a break in the wall that could only be a doorway.

Deciding that a long, hot soak was exactly what he needed, he moved toward the opening, loosening his cravat as he went. Once he was beyond the inner wall, he not only heard the underground spring that supplied the bath, he also smelled it, though the aroma was quite mild compared to the springs at many of the fashionable spas.

The small mosaic tiles that had once adorned the floor were gone, leaving only the moss-covered earth, which felt springy beneath his feet. Fortunately, the pool appeared intact, and the steam rising from the hot water prompted Harrison to hurry removing his clothing.

There was only the one pool, but the rectangle was at least forty feet long, and it was divided in the center by a half wall, possibly so the Roman officers could pretend they were not actually bathing with the foot soldiers. Not caring which end he used, Harrison laid his clothes as far from the edge of the pool as possible, then slipped quietly over the side, where deliciously hot water welcomed him.

Within moments the heat began to relax his calves and thighs. Harrison wanted to be submerged so the heat could work on the tired muscles of his back and shoulders; unfortunately, the water reached only to his waist, and many of the tiles were missing from the bottom of the pool, making sitting out of the question. Not one to give up easily, he decided to swim around the half wall to see if perhaps the water was deeper there.

In no hurry, he swam slowly, without making much of a splash, and as he rounded the half wall, his hand touched something that felt like human fingers. Not at all certain the fingers belonged to a living creature, Harrison snatched his hand back just as someone emitted a gasp, then quickly sank below the surface of the water.

The fingers were both human and alive, and they belonged to Charlotte Pelham, who had been floating on her back. She righted herself immediately, sputtering and pushing her hair out of her eyes; then, while treading water, she turned so she could see who had touched her.

"What are you—"

"What—"

They spoke at once, then fell silent. Since it was apparent they had both thought they were alone, explanations were unnecessary. But heaven help him! he wished she had not been there, swimming in the moonlight like some mythical siren from the sea.

"Forgive me, Miss Pelham. I had no wish to invade your privacy."

Though most of her was beneath the water, Harrison let his gaze wander over as much of her as he could see. Her black hair was unbound and completely wet, and the thick strands stuck to the sides of her face and neck, and fell across her bare shoulders in a way that made him long to reach out and touch every place the wet strands touched.

Not that her shoulders were completely bare. Thin, white cotton sleeves bunched at the tops of her arms, telling him she was swimming in her shift. Remembering that he swam in nothing at all, Harrison was careful to tread water.

"I had no idea anyone would be here," he said. "I will go."

"No," she said. "I will go. I have been here for at least half an hour."

"But I do not wish to run you off, especially since you were here first."

"Which is exactly why you deserve a turn. Believe me, another five minutes and my skin will be as wrinkled as a dried currant."

If there was one thing Harrison did *not* want to think about at that moment, it was Charlotte Pelham's skin! He was having a hard enough time not letting his mind wander to the shift that would by now be thoroughly transparent.

"I will go," he said agin.

"Do not be foolish," she said, and this time she chuckled, the sound echoing softly against the tile walls of the pool. "This is, after all, a *public* bath. At least, it was built as such. Why must either of us leave?"

If she could read his mind, she would not ask that question!

"Why, indeed?" he said.

Why? He knew perfectly well why. Because he was naked and up to his neck in warm water, opposite a woman who for all practical purposes was as naked as he. And she was within an arm's reach!

"I will go," he said.

He had turned to leave when she touched his shoulder. "Oh, Harrison?" she cooed.

She had to choose *now* to use his name! And with that teasing quality in her voice! "What?" he said, looking straight ahead, not daring to turn back to face her.

He was totally unprepared for what happened next. Uttering a cry worthy of one of the ancient Romans about to attack the enemy, Charlotte put both her hands on Harrison's shoulders. Seconds later, she jumped, using all her weight to push him beneath the water. When he emerged again, coughing and sputtering like a half-drowned puppy, she was swimming toward the shallow end of the pool. Peter had been right. She swam like a fish, and unless Harrison was much mistaken, she was laughing.

"Sorry," she called when she reached the end of the pool. "I could not resist."

"You took unfair advantage, madam, and well you know it!"

"Of course," she replied.

"If you wanted to water wrestle, you had only to tell me. I would have been happy to oblige. Come back now, and we will try for two out of three."

"Oh, no," she said, laughing again. "I am persuaded you would be much too embarrassed if I should best you a second time."

If they had been on land, he would have been obliged to make her prove the validity of that threat. As it was, she chose that moment to put her hands on the edge of the pool and push herself up and out of the water. The instant he saw her standing in the moonlight, her wet shift as near transparent as made no difference, he could not think clearly. His mind seemed incapable of focusing on anything but her figure.

A gentleman would have turned his back, giving her some privacy, but when the yellow-white moonlight glistened on the wet shift, revealing every curve of her lithe, slender body, Harrison could not look away. Not if his life had depended on it. No man could have, for Charlotte Pelham was every inch a woman, and every inch was magnificent!

Charlotte pushed herself up and out of the pool, and after the marvelous spring-heated water the air felt especially cold. She had brought her blanket with her, and now she grabbed it and wrapped it around her, happy to have the warmth of the rough wool. She had also brought her spare shift, but with Harrison in the pool, perhaps watching her, she dared not even think of disrobing. She would search out a private place later to change. For now, she merely turned and waved.

"Good night," she called. "Sweet dreams."

He mumbled something unintelligible, almost as if he was thinking about something else, and Charlotte bit back the disappointment she felt, knowing that he had already dismissed her from his thoughts. She sighed. What a fool she had been. For a moment, when he had first touched her hand, she had thought he knew she was in the pool and had come to enjoy the deliciously warm water with her.

What a laugh on her, for he had been surprised to discover her there. Surprised and, so it seemed, not at all pleased. She had been obliged to offer to leave. What else could she do? And yet, the entire time she had been swimming away from him, she had secretly hoped he would call her back, ask her stay awhile. It would have been wonderful, swimming in the moonlight with the man she loved.

Chapter Fourteen

For many people, the principal attraction of the North York Moors was their vastness, the seemingly unending space, but for Charlotte there was so much more to admire. In summer, the sunsets were spectacular, displaying every color imaginable, from palest gold to the most glorious purples. And not to be outdone, the winter evenings offered a sky alive with diamond-bright stars—stars whose twinkling lights appeared close enough to gather in one's hand. Whatever the season, for Charlotte there was always something more—a sort of timeless serenity those who were living shared with the spirits of the ancient people who had crossed the moors untold centuries ago.

High. Wild. Desolate. Unforgettable. They all described the North York Moors—moors where the brothers of the olden monasteries had erected stone crosses to guide travelers who lost their way in the often featureless landscape. Yet there were also the glorious surprises—surprises not unlike the one that awaited the ramblers on Saturday, the thirteenth day of their tour.

They had covered perhaps eight miles during the morning hours, and had decided to stop for their midday meal once they reached the Dove River. It being the last week in May, Charlotte knew what to expect, but she said nothing. There would be time enough to speak once the group had crossed the plain stone bridge that spanned one of the smaller tributaries of the Dove.

When the party reached the arch of the bridge, which allowed them to see the land on the other side of the water, there was a collective gasp, for on the riverbank, as far as the eye could see, was an immense colony of wild daffodils. The delicate, cuplike flowers, which were a mixture of white, palest yellow, and canary, stood on tall, slender green stems that swayed softly in the afternoon breeze.

"Oh, my," Russell Thorne said.

"Rather," Lawrence Vinton added.

For once, Colonel Fitzgibbon had nothing of his own or anyone else's to say; he merely gazed speechlessly at nature's display.

While everyone drank their fill of the unexpected beauty and breathed the heavenly perfume of literally thousands of flowers, a meadow pipit filled the air with its soft, musical song.

"Beautiful," Harrison Montgomery said softly.

For just an instant, Charlotte had thought he meant her. The assumption was foolish beyond permission, of course, for the veriest ninnyhammer would know he referred to the wild daffodils. "Yes," she said, "the flowers are lovely."

"Those, too," he said.

Before she could ask him what he meant by such a remark, Russell Thorne claimed her attention so he could tell her about the many butterflies that would soon be flitting around the flowers. "Vibrant painted ladies," he said, "as well as delicate clouded yellows and long-tail blues, even swallowtails. Hundreds and hundreds of them, with colors so lovely they fairly rival the flowers."

"Most interesting," Charlotte said, not at all sure what he was talking about.

"I thought you would want to know, Miss Pelham."

"Yes, yes. Of course I do."

What she *really* wanted to know was why Harrison had chosen to utter that one word. Was it meant for the flowers? Or could it be— No. No! She would not delude herself, for that way lay disaster. She was in love with Harrison Montgomery; she had admitted that much to herself, but as long as that was all she did, she could return to Lancashire with some pride. If she let herself see hidden meaning where none existed, she would carry home a broken heart.

The man had joined the tour for reasons of his own, and those reasons had nothing to do with her. In two days' time he, like everyone else, would bid her farewell and return to his normal life—a life she knew nothing about. And in all likelihood, she would never know anything about it, for after Monday she would never see Harrison Montgomery again.

Many times that afternoon, while they ate their midday meal on the banks of the Dove River, and afterward, she looked Harrison's way. Unfortunately, she did not get another chance to speak with him until just before they reached the final inn of their tour. They had been climbing gradually, and had finally reached a point where they could look down on what Charlotte considered the most spectacular valley of the cross-country walk.

The valley, which her father had claimed was cut eons ago by torrents of glacial meltwater, contained a forest of mixed conifer trees so lush and green they were a feast for the eyes. But even more dramatic than the forest was the waterfall on the far hillside. Halfway down, spewing from a deep cleft in the hill, was a fall of white water whose spray misted out for what seemed miles, and any time the sun shone, there was a rainbow above the spray.

This was, in effect, the scenic climax of their trip,

for after this they would traverse mostly meadows and villages. As if sensing the importance of the moment, everyone stopped where they were to take in the breathtaking panorama. No one spoke, and though there were birds soaring between the hillsides and sheep grazing in distant pastures, if they made any sound, it was lost in the distant roar of the falling water.

Charlotte was about to give the signal for the walk to continue when she felt someone grab her arm and give a rather urgent tug. "Come," Peter shouted into her ear. "Mr. Montgomery has been injured."

For a moment, Charlotte's heart ceased to beat. *Harrison injured? Please heaven, no!*

Visions flashed through her mind of the man she loved lying at the bottom of the steep hill, with terrible injuries or worse, and without stopping to think that her haste might give rise to embarrassing speculation, she pushed past Peter and ran back up the trail. For the time it took to run the fifty yards or so, Charlotte did not take a breath. Not until she saw Harrison sitting on the ground, his handkerchief held to his left temple, did she breathe again.

After falling to her knees beside him, she spoke directly into his ear. "Wh . . . what happened?"

"A rock," he replied, lifting the handkerchief so she could see the cut just in front of his ear and the blood he had been trying to stanch. "It came from up there." He pointed to a spot a dozen feet above them where the trail had forked. "I did not hear anything, of course, for the rushing water covered any footfalls. Nevertheless, I am convinced the rock was thrown."

Sparing a moment to look around, Charlotte saw one fist-sized rock, grayish with a telltale spot of red. Harrison's blood. There were no other stones lying about to indicate a possible natural rock slide, just the single stone, tossed by person or persons unknown. "Why you?" she asked.

Harrison shook his head, but he regretted the action immediately. The rock had hit him quite hard, and the entire right side of his face throbbed. "I was the last man on the trail. Perhaps the choice of target was more logistical than personal."

He could tell from the narrowing of her dark eyes that Charlotte did not appreciate his humor at a time like this. In fact, she was angry, though whether her ire was directed at him or the rock thrower, he could not tell. "I want to know something," she said, speaking slowly, her mouth so close to his ear he could feel her warm breath. "And I want an honest answer."

He stared at her for a moment, not sure he wanted to give her carte blanche with his most private thoughts. While he searched her face, however, her lips quivered, making her appear unbelievably vulnerable, and in that moment he knew he could not refuse her anything. "Ask what you will."

"Why did you join the tour?"

A day ago he might not have answered, but now there was no point in keeping his quest a secret. Jonathan was *her* brother, and Peter was not his. Harrison had nothing to gain by his silence. Leaning close enough for her to hear him, he said, "I was searching for my brother."

She pulled back, and the surprise on her face told him that whatever she had expected, it had not been that. "Where is he? Your brother, I mean."

"If I knew that, I would not be searching for him."

She ignored his sarcasm. "Is he lost?"

"Only to me, for I have not seen him in twelve years."

*   *   *

As soon as they arrived at the Wounded Hart Inn, Charlotte cleaned the cut on Harrison's cheek, then applied a dab of ointment and a sticking plaster, all with a steady hand. By the time she had changed for dinner, however, reaction had set in and she had little appetite. What if the rock thrower had been more accurate? Her stomach churned from the very thought of what could so easily have happened.

Once seated at the pretty oak table in the private parlor, she managed to drink some of the soup of baby fennel, and she even tried a little of the soft goat cheese served with a tangy oat biscuit. Even so, it was out of the question for her to swallow so much as a bite of the roasted breast of goose, marinated with stout, or the bread-and-butter pudding with raspberry sauce.

Harrison might have been killed, and she did not know why, no more than she knew why all the other accidents had happened. Struck by a sudden, depressing thought, she turned to Harrison, who sat to her left at the table. "You are not planning to leave now, are you? You will continue all the way to Robin Hood's Bay with us, will you not?"

"Of course. Why do you ask?"

Charlotte sighed, feeling as if a crushing load had been lifted from her heart. "After the accident at the gorge, the Richardsons left us. Then Lady Griswall went home. Now *you* are injured. I was afraid . . . I mean, I just thought . . ." She paused, realizing that everyone at the table was listening.

"Do not worry," he said. "I am not so easy to get rid of."

Lawrence Vinton raised his wineglass in salute. "Good for you, sir."

Andrew Vinton, who had met them at the Wounded Hart Inn, looking a bit fatigued, but without the first explanation for his absence the evening before, raised his glass as well.

The colonel was far more interested in the roast goose than in the conversation, but obviously feeling he must add something, he said "Faint heart ne'er won fair maid." Since he followed this seeming non sequitur by stuffing a rather large bite of fowl in his mouth, his part of the conversation was apparently at an end.

"I cannot think," Wilfred Bryce said, "that anyone would find my opinion of the least interest. But be that as it may, I wonder, Mr. Montgomery, if it is altogether wise for you to travel? I understand your servant has caught up with us at last with your Tilbury, so you would not be alone if you decided to remain here at the inn for a time, until you were completely recuperated."

"He was hit by a rock," Jonathan said, undisguised scorn in his voice, "not run through with a sword. If he feels he cannot walk the final day, he can ride in the wagon with me."

"I thank you both," Harrison said, "for your interest in my welfare. However, I am perfectly capable of finishing the tour."

Charlotte was immeasurably cheered to hear him say so. "Besides," she added, "tomorrow being the Sabbath, he has all day to rest."

He looked at her then, his gray eyes filled with a teasing light that sent little flutters of sensation all along her skin. "Not *all* day, Miss Pelham. I had hoped that you would allow me to show you a bit of the village. Benizur informs me there is a gentleman's establishment nearby, with a gallery containing some very impressive portraiture. The owner of the house is away for most of the year, so for a modest sum, the housekeeper will give interested parties a tour of the gallery."

At the invitation, Charlotte's heart felt light enough to float right out of her body, and she discovered within herself a sudden desire to increase her knowledge of portraiture. "I should be delighted to go," she said. "Directly after chapel."

"Er, of course, ma'am. After chapel."

The vicar was not in attendance at the small, but impressive Norman church, with its thick flint and mortar walls, and in that worthy gentleman's absence, the curate had the good sense to limit his sermon to half an hour. For that reason, it was only just past noon when Charlotte and Harrison climbed aboard his maroon-and-gold Tilbury, settled themselves comfortably on the black leather seat, and tooled down the village High Street.

As far as Charlotte was concerned, life could offer her no more treat than this. The sun was shining, she was riding in a gig that was the height of fashion, and best of all, she was sitting beside the man she loved. While the pretty roan trotted through the village and out onto the country lane, she forgot all her worries, allowing herself to enjoy the moment. "Am I to assume," she said, turning so she could watch Harrison's expert handling of the ribbons, "that you are an admirer of fine portraiture?"

He chuckled. "I am found out."

"Found out?"

"Yes, for I know nothing of art or artists."

"Nothing? Then why—"

"What I do know about," he said, "is a certain young lady who takes her position as guide much too seriously, obliging me to resort to subterfuge to get her alone for an hour or so."

Happily for the harmony of their drive, Charlotte found nothing to dislike in his confession. In fact, she rather liked the idea of being alone with Harrison, especially since tomorrow might well be the last time she ever saw him. Thinking of the end of the journey reminded her of the beginning, when he had blackmailed his way onto the tour, and she decided now was as good a time as any to discover his true motive. "You told me yesterday that your purpose in joining the tour was to find your brother."

"That is true."

"If I may ask, what made you think you would find him among the ramblers?"

"Not among the ramblers," he said. "I thought he might be either Jonathan or Peter."

"What!"

"My brother is fifteen, and when I saw him last, his hair and eyes were dark, not unlike those of Peter and your brother. It stood to reason that he would probably grow to look very much like those two lads."

"And you joined a tour simply because you caught sight of a pair of dark-eyed boys of fifteen?"

Harrison shook his head. "I was not quite that foolish, though now that I look back on all the blunders I made, I might just as well have been hunting mares' nests."

"I do not understand."

"How could you? Suffice it to say I have erred in every conceivable way."

He told her about following the lead to the Newsome family, then chasing after Charlotte's coach when he discovered that young Newsome was with her and her brother.

"And you did not think to ask Peter's name?"

"My blunders," he said, "are become legion."

"Well, at least that explains your rather noticeable interest in the boys. What I do not understand is why you did not simply tell one of them what you wanted."

"That, of course, is your fault."

"Mine!"

"Absolutely. I attempted to ask a few subtle questions before making my purpose known, but both lads were adamant about not disclosing the fact that you had invented brothers from here to Timbuktu."

The exaggeration was so outrageous Charlotte had to laugh. "I am not altogether certain where one may find Timbuktu, but I know for a fact that I have invented only two brothers."

"Only two? It may interest you to know, madam, that most people have never even invented *one*."

"Am I expected to apologize for the lack of imagination in *most* people?"

It was Harrison's turn to laugh. "Not at all. One might, of course, be forgiven for expecting you to apologize for the trouble your falsehood caused me."

"Then I do so."

"That is it? The extent of your apology?"

"I answer only for having told a falsehood. You must accept your own culpability for not being frank from the beginning." She said nothing for a moment; then she added quietly, "You could have just asked me. I would have told you what you wanted to know."

The humor had gone out of their banter, and once again Harrison felt that heaviness of heart he had experienced when Peter told him he was not adopted. "I wish I had asked you. I asked Peter, instead."

"You did? When?"

"Friday evening, when I walked Jonathan to the inn and brought Peter back to take his place."

"And what did Peter say?"

"He said that Jonathan is, actually, your brother and that the Newsomes are *his* real parents. The lad told me, as well, that he was not adopted."

"As to that, he is only partially correct."

Something in her voice made the breath catch in Harrison's throat, and sensing that he would want to give Charlotte his full attention, he pulled the roan over to the side of the lane and stopped the gig. At last, he turned to look at his companion. "What do you mean by 'partially correct'?"

"The squire and Mrs. Newsome are most truly Peter's father and mother. However, he was not born to them."

Not wanting to make another mistake, Harrison asked if she meant he was adopted.

"I am not privy to the formalities of it, you understand, but I would call it an adoption."

"Forgive me for asking, but how is it that you know something the lad does not know?"

"Simple. I remember when they brought him home to Burley. He probably does not. I was thirteen at the time, quite old enough to understand what was happening. My parents told me I was not to speak of it, there being people who do not approve of adoption, but I remember the first day I ever saw him. He was quite shy and rather small for his age. Not nearly as big as Jonathan, though there are only a few weeks' difference in their ages."

Harrison had at least a hundred questions, but fear of disappointment all but sealed his lips. Finally, he settled for just one question. "How old was the child when you first saw him?"

"As I said, I was thirteen. I am positive about that, for I had just had my birthday the week before, and I was riding Bess, the pony my father had given me as my present. Bess and I were galloping down the lane when I saw the squire's traveling coach enter the Newsome carriageway. They had Peter with them, and he was staring out the window of the coach as though he had no idea where he was or why he was there. I remembered his big, sad brown

eyes. Naturally, I could not even guess who he was,
but I waved to him just the same."

"And?" Barely concealing his impatience, Harrison
said, "How old was he at that time?"

"If I was thirteen, then he would have been four
years old."

Four. The boy was four. The same age as Timmy!

Harrison's hands fairly itched to turn the Tilbury
around and race back to the Wounded Hart Inn as
fast as the roan could carry them; instead, he forced
himself to exercise restraint. He had rushed from
London to Burley like a complete Bedlamite; then,
from Burley to St. Bee's Head in much the same manner. For once, it behooved him to act with caution.
The lad either did not remember that he was
adopted, or else he had convinced himself that it was
not so. Either way, it would be no kindness to insist
he accept something he had no wish to believe.

Slowly, Harrison turned the roan, and as he did
so, he asked Charlotte if she would mind forgoing
the viewing of the portraiture. "I would like to return
to the inn."

"Of course I do not mind about the portraits. However, I must warn you, I cannot let you badger Peter.
He may look almost grown, but he is not. His father—that is to say, the squire—trusted me to look
after his son, and though I can understand your desire to ask Peter all manner of questions, I think the
properest person to query is Squire Newsome."

She was right. The rational, perhaps even the ethi-
cal thing to do would be to wait until he could speak
to the man who was his brother's adopted parent.
No, his *possible* brother's parent. In Harrison's more
sensible moments, it was exactly what he had
planned to do. Still, the waiting would be difficult.
"Will you tell me just one more thing?"

"Yes," she replied. "If I can."

"My brother's name is Timmy. Do you ever remember hearing him called anything other than Peter?"

She shook her head. "I am sorry. He spoke very little when we first met him, and by the time he was comfortable with Jonathan and me, we had grown accustomed to calling him Peter. Similarly, I suppose he had become accustomed to answering to the name."

They rode for a time in silence; then Charlotte cleared her throat to gain his attention. "Now," she said, "may I ask *you* something?"

"By all means."

"Why do you want to find this brother? Do not misunderstand me. I have a brother of my own, one I love with all my heart, so I know why I would search for Jonathan."

"Then you already have your answer. I want to find Timmy for the same reasons you would want to find Jonathan if you had been separated from him. Timmy is my brother, and I love him. He is all the family I have left, and possibly all the family I will ever have."

"All you will ever—" A feeling of cold started in Charlotte's heart, then quickly spread through her body to her hands and her feet. "Why," she asked quietly, "do you think you might never have any more family than your brother? Have you no desire for a wife and perhaps children of your own?"

"A wife?" He shook his head. "I cannot think you would need to ask me that. Surely you, of all people, have noticed that I am, shall we say, a bit rough around the edges."

"Not so very rough," she said quietly.

"Rough enough. I went to sea far too young and stayed much too long. And as a result, my manners—if they can be called such—are far from gentlemanly. I learned much in those twelve years, and

while the majority of the lessons made me an effi-
cient businessman, I cannot think they would render
me an acceptable guest in a lady's drawing room."

"Upon my oath, sir, you are very harsh on yourself."

"I think not. A wise man knows both his strengths
and his weaknesses. Even so, I find I have high standards for a wife. Perhaps impossibly high standards.
And yet, I will not settle for less."

Impossibly high standards. Charlotte knew all too
well what that meant. Like most men, he wanted
a diamond of the first water, a beauty with social
connections and all the feminine graces. And if he
was as rich as Lady Griswall had implied, then he
could look as high as he liked for a wife.

The thought was like a knife through Charlotte's
heart. Though she had not realized it before, in some
private place deep inside her soul, she had hoped
that Harrison might eventually look her way. She
had thought that if only they had enough time together, he would come to love her . . . to want her
for his wife.

Too, too foolish! What man wanted a wife whose
only accomplishments were her ability to outride,
outshoot, and outswim any man she knew?

Charlotte bit back a sob that threatened to escape
her lips. She would not let herself cry! Not here. Not
now. There would be time enough for tears later.

"Do you think I should settle for less?" he asked.

The question surprised Charlotte into looking his
way. "No. Not at all. Definitely not!" She knew she
was protesting too much, but she could not stop herself. "Why should you settle for anything less than
the person you want? I . . . I know I never would.
If I cannot have the man I love, then I will take no
other."

"The man you—" He turned to stare at her, the

look on his face one of surprise. "I had not thought there was anyone special in your life. What I mean to say is, I can understand if there is someone. I had just never entertained the possibility."

Never entertained the possibility! Was she so undesirable? Charlotte was filled with mortification. Harrison did not love her, and as if that was not heartbreaking enough, he found it difficult to believe that anyone else would.

"Forgive me," he said, his voice sounding surprisingly flat, "but are . . . are you engaged, Miss Pelham?"

Pride, and pride alone, kept Charlotte's voice even. "Earlier, when I said you could have asked me, I meant you could have asked me about Peter. Peter, not me. And now, Mr. Montgomery, you have asked one question too many."

Chapter Fifteen

One question too many? It seemed to Harrison that he had asked one too few. And too late!

He had high standards right enough. So high they had all but turned him against the idea of marriage. He had been in earnest about his rough seaman's manners. He was no gentleman, and so far the only "ladies" who had shown any interest in becoming his wife had been far more enamored of his money than of him.

The woman who married him would be obliged to overlook much and accept much, like the fact that he wanted to become reacquainted with his brother. If possible, he wanted Timmy to live with him so they would have time to get to know each other again. There was no making up for the years they had lost, but there was always the chance that as adults they might become friends.

Harrison thought he had met the very woman who would understand his need to rebuild the relationship with his brother. She already loved Peter, and she did not appear to be put off by the fact that Harrison was not a nonpareil and never would be. He had even let himself believe there was a chance Charlotte Pelham could learn to love him, in spite of his drawbacks. And now, he discovered she loved another, was possibly already engaged to be married.

Damnation! Life had dealt Harrison some cruel

blows in the past, but none so unkind as this. How perverse of the fates to allow him to find the brother he had never stopped loving, only to lose the woman he thought he could love forever.

Dinner that evening was a rather quiet affair. Harrison, like Charlotte, was lost in private thought, and the four other men of the group appeared to have exhausted all the dining table civilities at their disposal. Perhaps their thoughts were concentrated on the next day and the final fifteen miles of the walk. Whatever the cause, the burden of conversation fell on Peter, Jonathan, and Lawrence Vinton, and such gambits as those three young men introduced centered on the relative merits of Oxford and Cambridge.

The next morning found the gentlemen no more talkative than they had been the evening before. In fact, they broke their fasts almost as strangers. If Charlotte's heart had not already suffered a devastating blow, she might have attempted to stir up the group a bit, scale the walls that were already being built between them as the time for parting grew near. Unfortunately, she had neither the time nor the inclination to fight against the inevitable end-of-the-party malaise.

Fortunately, the walk that had begun fourteen days earlier on the cliffs of the Irish Sea continued to unveil its marvels, and as the group rambled onward toward the wild coast of the North Sea, they found much to entertain them. Not the least of those entertainments was another stretch of Roman road, complete with culverts and even an occasional curbstone. Though the surface stones of the road had eroded, or perhaps been taken away by Yorkshiremen who had, in their turn, returned to the earth, there was still evidence of the Roman Legions.

Perhaps the most interesting site, however, was the flattened hilltop on which stood the three barrows. Even before the time of the Saxons, the ancient people had buried their dead in raised barrows formed by balancing large capstones on top of a circle of standing stones, then covering the whole with mounds of earth. Naturally, time had eroded the mounds, leaving only the standing stones, but even so, to find three at once—one long barrow and two small circular ones—was enough to pull even the most jaded rambler out of the doldrums.

At one point, Lawrence Vinton was certain he had stumbled upon a Roman campsite, but after the barrows, the more mature gentlemen were no longer interested in Roman ruins. Still, Lawrence and Peter would not be satisfied until they had made a thorough inspection of the site.

Harrison had been true to his word, and as far as Charlotte could tell, he had not pursued Peter with questions regarding his childhood. She had noticed, though, that he watched the lad whenever he thought he could do so without being observed. As well, Charlotte had seen Peter looking Harrison's way from time to time. And yet, neither one of them went out of their way to engage the other in conversation.

If anything, Peter appeared to have made a last-minute friend of Lawrence Vinton, and during the entire morning, Charlotte never saw one boy without seeing the other. For that reason, she did not become overly concerned when the pair did not join them immediately for the midday meal.

Harrison was the first to comment upon their absence. "Perhaps they found another Stonehenge," he said, his voice surprisingly indulgent. "When it comes to lads of that age, I suppose it is asking too much to expect cold roast beef and a bit of ginger-bread to be more interesting than a new discovery."

Andrew Vinton, who had never been separated from his younger brother, wasted no time in adding comments of his own, comments not nearly so approving. "No doubt found another Roman camp-site," the solicitor said. "Many's the time I have needed to give Lawrence a hint about forever boring others with his interest in the Roman invaders."

"At least one thing is certain," Russell Thorne observed. "Your brother has discovered a kindred spirit in Peter."

"Birds of a feather," Colonel Fitzgibbon said.

"I remember seeing them," Wilfred Bryce said. "If you will trust me with the commission, Miss Pelham, I will be happy to walk back and tell them to step lively. Or, I can show you the way, if you feel you must tell them yourself. Which, of course, I will certainly understand."

As usual, Bryce had phrased his question so that almost any way Charlotte chose to answer, it would sound as though she did not trust him. And yet, for some reason a shiver went up her spine, and in that moment she decided she would very much prefer to fetch Peter and Lawrence herself. "Thank you, Mr. Bryce, but there is no need for you to trouble yourself. Only tell me the last landmark. I am persuaded I will find those two."

"As you wish, ma'am. It was about half a mile back, rather near that final barrow. They were heading toward a winding footpath leading up a wooded hill."

Deciding to go that moment, Charlotte left her haversack on the ground, then hurried back down the path they had just traveled. Within seconds she was out of sight of the others. Not that she noticed, for she was much too busy trying to determine why Bryce's comments had sent a chill up her spine. She did not like the man; she readily admitted that much, at least to herself, and it had nothing to do with him being a clerk. What it had to do with she could not say, but she could not rid her thoughts of that other time she had felt uncomfortable in his presence—the night at the hot spring, where the group had slept under the stars.

At that time, Bryce had expressed his curiosity about the many problems that had beset the tour. While restating his claim of being a novice, he had planted the idea in Charlotte's mind that someone might be deliberately trying to keep her from finishing the tour. "To prove that you cannot do the job," he had added.

Charlotte had tried to put the idea from her head, but several times the clerk's words had come back to her. It was a foolish notion, of course, for no one had anything to gain by her failing as a guide. No one, that is, except perhaps the man who did not get the job leading this first cross-country walking tour.

Preposterous, of course! And yet, a possible four hundred pounds in one season was a great deal of money. Very few men earned that large a sum, and people committed all manner of transgressions for money. She was living proof of that. Had she not gained the chance to lead the first tour by telling a falsehood?

Because she was a woman, there was every possibility the travel agency would not give her the job, no matter how well she had done. Of course, the other guide would not know that. He would, however, know that she was required to arrive with at least five of the original party.

Naturally, he would have no way of knowing how many people might complete the course, not without having a cohort on the tour to ensure that fewer than five actually reached Robin Hood's Bay. Or, he could be on the tour himself!

The very idea turned that shiver going up Charlotte's back into a figurative plunge into a frozen lake. Her skin felt ice-cold, and before she could stop herself, she had turned to look behind her, uncharacteristically nervous.

This was foolish beyond permission, for another guide could not possibly be one of the party. He just could not be. Except that the longer Charlotte toyed with the idea, the more it helped explain the series of mishaps. After all, there could be only three explanations for all those "accidents." One was bad luck, the other was poor leadership, and the third was a saboteur.

Bad luck she ruled out immediately. Except for acts of nature, she believed people made their own luck.

As for leadership, she was a good guide! In fact, she was an excellent guide, and thoroughly competent. No one knew the trails better than she, and very few people had more experience in the out-of-doors. She was skilled, confident, and resourceful, and though she always strove to go that one more inch to improve herself, she was never reckless.

So how, then, had the accidents happened? Or more to the point, *who* had made them happen? The colonel? One of the Vinton brothers? Wilfred Bryce? Russell Thorne? Harrison?

No, no! Not Harrison. She refused to entertain that doubt again.

Without really thinking about where she was going, she spotted the winding footpath Wilfred Bryce had told her about. It appeared to lead directly up a hill toward a small, wooded area, and as she turned onto the path, she searched her mind for clues to the saboteur's identity. She considered the latest incident first, beginning with Friday, day twelve, when Harrison had been hit by a rock. It was certainly no accident, but he had seen no one. He might almost have been there alone.

Since that incident offered no proof at all of the saboteur's identity, Charlotte went on to the previous accident, which happened on Thursday. In that instance, at least, there had been no attempt to conceal the identity of the perpetrator, for when Wilfred Bryce kicked Jonathan in the shin, her brother had been walking with Lawrence Vinton, in full view of the colonel. And heaven knew, Bryce had apologized profusely for his clumsiness.

Very unsaboteurlike behavior!

As for the day Charlotte stepped into the hollow log containing the beehive, that certainly could not have been planned, nor could it be blamed on anyone but her. She had been careless. No mystery there. At the time, she was angry with Harrison and was not paying attention to what she was doing.

In fact, she had been fortunate that Harrison was there to pull her out of the log so quickly. A few seconds' delay and she could have been badly stung. Bryce had helped as well, lifting her up the bank. That was the day she had discovered that the clerk was more muscular than he looked, and surprisingly strong.

Then there was the episode of the adder in Lady Griswall's haversack. Though that cruel trick was no accident, it had resulted in reducing the number of paying ramblers, something the "other" guide would want to see happen. In this instance, however, Russell Thorne had volunteered to watch the adder to see it did not get close to her ladyship. Thorne. Now there was a man with a lot of muscles. As well, he was knowledgeable about flora and fauna, and he was an experienced climber.

Of course, Andrew Vinton was muscular as well.

Charlotte remembered that it was Vinton and Peter who had pulled Dora Richardson up when she had fallen over the edge of the gorge. Naturally, Bryce had been the acknowledged hero, for he had been the one to initially save Dora by grabbing her wrist and hanging on until Peter and Vinton took over, but—

No! Something was not quite right about that memory. Something had always been wrong!

All along Charlotte had thought it out of character for an intelligent, agile young woman like Dora Richardson to suddenly lose her footing, and equally strange that the man who saved her was the clumsiest man in the group. Far too clumsy to catch a falling woman by her wrist, maintain his own balance so he did not follow her over the side, then hang on to her until others came to take his place. *Two others!*

As she brought to mind the picture of Wilfred Bryce at the edge of the gorge, Charlotte recalled him on his knees in the dusty red soil, holding Dora's wrist with his right hand. One hand, not two. Now that she thought of it, that had always puzzled her. Vinton and Peter had used both hands to pull Dora up, and Harrison had used both hands to pull her the final few inches to safety. Only Bryce had managed with just the one hand.

One hand. His right hand, for his left was down by his side, the fingers curled around something—something to which he clung with all his might. It was a knife, or a spike, something that had been plunged securely into the ground to keep the alleged hero from going over the rim just like the young woman he had pushed.

And he *had* pushed her! Charlotte was convinced of that fact. But why?

The moment she asked herself the question, she knew the answer. Dora was small, with delicate bones, and she probably did not weigh much over six stone. Certainly no more than a man of Bryce's height and muscles could handle. All he had to do was frighten her, and she and her husband would leave the tour. Like Charlotte, he had probably decided the young couple were the least likely to finish the entire walk, so they were his first two victims.

Lady Griswall practically chose herself as the third to leave by revealing her vulnerability—her fear of reptiles. Bryce must have doubled back after Russell Thorne left the adder alive, then killed the snake and waited for his chance to put it in her ladyship's haversack.

What a cruel, cruel man. Charlotte was thinking she should be grateful he had only kicked Jonathan in the shin, when it occurred to her that her brother had not been the intended victim. He must have unwittingly stepped in the way at the last second. Bryce had meant to injure Lawrence, for with one brother unable to walk, the other brother would be obliged to quit the tour as well, leaving only Bryce, Harrison, the colonel, and Thorne. Without five paying walkers, Charlotte would have forfeited her pay for this tour and lost any possibility of further employment as the agency's guide.

Wilfred Bryce. What sort of person would frighten two respectable ladies on holiday, and injure a young man, just on the chance he might win a job paying a possible four hundred pounds per annum?

Charlotte had only just asked herself that question when she got her answer, for she had reached the wooded area, and just ahead of her, almost concealed by the shade from a large oak tree, stood the villain himself, a coil of rope in his hand. The toadeating smile was gone from his face, and in its place was a look of pure hatred. She did not bother asking him how he had gotten there before her; instead, she inquired after Peter and Lawrence. "Where are the boys?"

"I have no idea. Nor do I care."

"If you have hurt them in any way, I vow I will—"

"Threats, Miss Pelham?" The servile voice was gone, and the words came out almost in a snarl. "Most unwise of you, for you would do well not to provoke me further."

"Provoke you! I am more apt to report you to the authorities. At the very least, I will inform the gentlemen at Bonaventure Tours of the mayhem you have caused. I feel certain they will know how to deal with you."

"First," he said, shifting the coil of rope to his other hand, then taking a step toward her, "I doubt anyone would believe you, since you got this commission by lying. Furthermore, an incompetent guide would naturally try to place the blame for his—or her—mistakes on someone else."

Charlotte took a step back, but he countered by taking another toward her. "Secondly," he said, "for you to say anything to anyone, you will need to leave this place, a circumstance I mean to make as difficult as possible."

Not leave? Hoping to conceal how much his words had frightened her, she said, "What do you mean by 'difficult'? Surely you do not believe you can just tie me to a tree and walk away."

He shook his head. "Nothing so obvious, I assure you."

"Then what—"

"I mean to tie you up, right enough, but to ensure that you are restrained for at least the next few days, I mean to leave you in a nice, quiet barrow I chanced upon earlier. One where the earth has not completely eroded from the rock structure. You will be safe from the elements there, and if you listen sharply, before too long you should hear some passersby."

He laughed, though the sound had little humor in it. "Of course, there is no guarantee that a passerby would wish to investigate a cry for help coming from an ancient burial mound. Still, you would be well-advised to try your luck."

A barrow. The very idea of being bound hand and foot and stashed in a burial mound was enough to make anyone's flesh crawl, and Charlotte's was no exception. And yet, she was no hothouse flower, and she would not submit quietly to such treatment. Let him try it! If Wilfred Bryce meant to tie her up, he would have to catch her first.

For years she had been pitting her skills against those of males, but all too aware of how strong Bryce was, Charlotte doubted she would get the better of him in a hand-to-hand struggle. Still, if she could make a break for it, she might outrun him. She was weighing her chances for doing just that when she thought she saw movement of some kind off to the right.

Thinking it might be Peter and Lawrence Vinton, she began to talk rather loud, to warn them of the danger. "Why are you doing this, Bryce? What have I ever done to you to make you wish to harm me?"

"What have you done?" Those small, muddy green eyes that had once put Charlotte in mind of a fox darkened with the man's anger. "You took the job I wanted, that's what. And you a female." He said the last word as though it left a nasty taste in his mouth. "Females have no business taking a job away from a man. It's the same as stealing the bread from his table."

Charlotte was now certain she saw someone circling slowly, stealthily around behind Bryce. Hoping to keep him distracted, she continued. "But what if the female needs to support herself? What if she needs to put bread on her own table?"

"Bah! Females got it easy in this life. It's men that have it hard. You women got nothing to do but keep yourselves looking pretty 'til some fool man fancies you enough to marry you. Then, if the man don't shower you with geegaws 'til he's not got sixpence in his pocket, you'll run off with the first bloke who catches your eye. Harlots, the lot of you!"

Not at all interested in his warped view of the entire female sex, Charlotte asked him how he expected to explain her absence to the group. "Surely you do not think they would leave without me?"

"I have that all planned. I'll tell them you decided to return to the last inn to see for yourself that your brother got away all right, and that you asked me to lead the walk for the final stage. They are all tired and ready for the trip to end, so they'll not balk at following me. And that way, it'll be me who delivers the group to Robin Hood's Bay."

"I would not be too sure of that," Peter said. The lad stood not more than three feet behind Bryce.

Surprised that someone had snuck up on him, Bryce spun around. When he saw that it was only Peter, he laughed, the sound harsh and derisive. "You thinking to stop me, boy?"

"If he does not, I will."

Since the second voice belonged to Harrison Montgomery, who had approached from the side, through the woods, Charlotte breathed a sigh of relief. Bryce might try to harm Peter, but he would think twice about challenging a man of Harrison's size, especially when that man held a long, thin dagger in his hand. It was the same dangerous-looking knife Harrison had used to remove the bee's stinger from Charlotte's neck. At the time, she had thought it an unusual item to be wearing on one's person during a simple walking tour, but now she was obliged to modify her thinking on the subject, especially when Bryce dropped the rope and pulled a knife of his own.

Moments later, the man spun around and grabbed Peter, wrapping his arm around the boy's neck and pressing the edge of the blade against his throat. "Drop your weapon," he said, "or you will force me to harm the boy."

Harrison dropped the dagger immediately. "There is no need for this foolishness to end in bloodshed," he said, his voice quiet, placating. "Just let the lad go, and you can walk away from here a rich man."

"Do you take me for a fool? I let the boy go, and you'll jump me."

"No. I will not move from this spot. I swear it. Just do not hurt the lad. You can even have Miss Pelham tie my hands and feet with that rope so I cannot jump you."

Bryce looked from Harrison to Charlotte and back, as though trying to decide what he should do.

"Ten thousand pounds," Harrison said. "Just name your bank, and the money will be there waiting for you within two days."

From the look on Bryce's face, it was clear he wanted to accept the offer. "How can I trust you'll do what you say?"

It was unclear to Charlotte if Bryce knew how hard he was pressing the knife against Peter's throat, or if he was just too nervous to realize what he was doing. Either way, as she watched in horror, a thin line of blood appeared, and red began to trickle down the lad's neck.

Charlotte gasped, but Harrison did not move. "Twenty thousand," he said quickly. "You have my word on it."

"What's the word of a man who's got nothing to lose?"

Harrison swallowed; then as if coming to a decision, he said, "I have everything to lose, believe me. The lad is my brother."

Charlotte could not say who was more surprised by the confession, Bryce or Peter. However, it was the former who spoke. "Your brother? You're trying to bamboozle me. If he's your brother, why did Miss Pelham say he was hers?"

"Inventing brothers is one of her pastimes. Besides, she did not know he was *my* brother, and that I had been looking for him. I came on this trip for no other reason than to find him."

"You're lying," Bryce said. Straightening suddenly, he took two steps back, pulling Peter with him.

"Stop!" Harrison said. His voice was no longer placating, but filled with iron resolve, and so cold it fairly froze Charlotte to the spot. "Unhand the boy this instant," he said, "and the twenty thousand pounds is yours, but take one more step, and on my oath that money will go to the first man who brings me proof of your murder."

Sweat popped out on Bryce's forehead. Clearly he did not know what to do, so he tightened his arm around Peter's neck and asked him if Harrison was, indeed, his brother? "And the truth, boy, or I'll make you sorry you even thought of lying to me."

Peter clutched at the powerful arm cutting off his air supply. He had trouble drawing breath, but he made a valiant effort to speak. "I . . . I . . . Perhaps."

"Damn you!" Harrison said. "The lad does not remember me, and choking the life out of him will not get you the answer you seek."

Then, in a softer tone, he spoke directly to Peter, attempting to jog the boy's memory. "You once had a rocking horse that you loved dearly. The day I left for India, you fell off that horse and cut yourself behind the left ear. The nurse, Nanny Clark, put a court plaster on the cut; then to stop your tears I swung you up on my shoulders so you could see yourself in the looking glass. Later, when I was in the traveling coach, you and the nurse came out to the carriageway and waved good-bye to me."

"Well?" Bryce said, momentarily tightening the arm around Peter's neck. "Is all of that true?"

Peter had listened carefully the entire time Harrison was speaking, and now his brow was furrowed, as if he was trying hard to remember. "I think I remember a rocking horse," he said. "Was . . . Was his name Sonny?"

Harrison inhaled deeply, as if he, too, found it difficult to breathe. "That was not the horse's name. That was what you called me. I am Sonny," Harrison said, His voice so hoarse he was obliged to swallow before he could continue. "I am your brother."

For a moment there was complete silence; then Charlotte heard someone call her name. "Miss Pelham?" It was Russell Thorne. "Where are you?"

"Lawrence!" Mr. Andrew Vinton yelled. "If you are hiding someplace, be warned, I am not amused. Come out now."

"I am here," the younger Mr. Vinton replied, his voice coming form somewhere in the woods. "But I cannot come out. Mr. Bryce is up here, and he has a knife."

"The devil you say!" Immediately, Charlotte heard the thud of footfalls on dry earth as Andrew Vinton ran up the hill, Mr. Thorne following close behind.

She was not the only one to hear the men's approach, for Wilfred Bryce's eyes had grown large with fright. He had the look of a cornered rat, and like a rat, his reaction was less rational decision and more survival instinct. After muttering a curse, he shoved Peter with all his force, pushing him directly at Harrison, and in Harrison's attempt to catch the lad, they both fell back, rolling partway down the hill until their descent was stopped by a protruding tree root.

While Bryce ran, disappearing into the woods, Charlotte hurried down to see if Harrison and Peter were all right. Harrison was already on his feet, having sustained no more than a few scratches on his face and neck, but Peter lay on the ground, unmoving, his face unnaturally pale.

Charlotte would have gone to Peter's assistance, had Harrison not stopped her by scooping his brother into his arms and lifting him off the ground. "Peter," he said, his voice so thick the single word was almost unintelligible.

To Charlotte's relief, Peter moaned, then opened his eyes. "Sonny?"

"Do not worry, lad, I have you, and no one will ever hurt you again. You have my promise on it."

"Sonny?" he said again.

"Yes, lad?"

"Take me with you."

Tears glistened in Harrison's eyes, making the gray shine like polished silver. "Do not worry, Timmy. This time you go where I go."

Chapter Sixteen

Jonathan Pelham waited for his sister and the party of ramblers at a plain little inn with a stone facade and mullioned windows. The inn's primary appeal was not its looks, but its location, for it was situated on one of the cliffs overlooking the rocky reef of Robin Hood's Bay. Not that the dramatic scenery was of any interest to Mr. Hiram Simpkins, the gentleman from Bonaventure Tours of London. Neither the rocky shoreline nor the North Sea waves that crashed against it beckoned Mr. Simpkins, who was much too eager to know the outcome of this maiden cross-country tour.

Jonathan, like Benizur, played least in sight, not wanting to answer any of the questions put to him by Mr. Simpkins, preferring to leave all explanations to Charlotte. Even so, Jonathan was surprised to see only his sister and four of the original walkers enter the inn late that afternoon. As for the representative from the travel agency, that gentleman was aghast at the small, quiet group.

"Where," Hiram Simpkins asked, his plump face turning dangerously red, "are the other people who signed up for the tour? There were supposed to be eight of them. And where the deuce is the guide, Mr. Charles Pelham?"

Charlotte shook the surprised gentleman's hand, told him she would speak with him in just a moment, then went directly to Benizur, giving him the message Harrison had asked her to deliver. "Mr. Montgomery wishes you to bring the Tilbury to a little village called Wensley, which is some five miles west of here. He is there with Peter Newsome, who has sustained an injury."

"Peter hurt?" Jonathan said. "I vow, Charlie, this tour was cursed."

"Charlie?" The complexion of the gentleman from Bonaventure went a shade redder. "Surely you are not *Charles* Pelham."

"No, sir, I am not. I am Miss Charlotte Pelham. For the past fortnight, I have guided the walkers from St. Bee's Head to this spot."

"You! But . . . but . . . madam, I—"

"I beg your pardon, sir, for the deception, but it was I who wrote you the letters. Though my credentials are as I stated them in the letters, there is no one called Charles Pelham."

Even after everything had been explained to Mr. Simpkins, including Bryce's villainy, and after all four of the remaining ramblers had declared themselves more than satisfied with their adventure and their guide, the gentleman from Bonaventure Tours would not even discuss the matter of future employment for Charlotte. "Madam," he said, "it must be obvious to anyone with common sense that such a venture is beyond a female's capabilities."

"But, sir," Russell Thorne said, "Miss Pelham has proven herself more than capable of leading the cross-country walk."

"Without question," Colonel Fitzgibbon added. "Had my own doubts earlier, but a very competent female, I assure you. Nonsensical to judge a book by its cover, my good man."

Mr. Simpkins held his tongue during Russell Thorne's remark, after all, Mr. Thorne was a gentleman, but he turned the full extent of his anger on the colonel. "You, sir, are an old windbag, and I will thank you to keep your opinions to yourself and your nose out of my business."

It was not to be wondered at that such animadversion would raise the ire of the rest of the party, who had over the course of the fortnight become rather fond of the military gentleman—platitudes and all— and they all rushed to his defense. Poor Mr. Simpkins, disappointed at the outcome of the tour and feeling as though he had been tricked and cheated and was now being attacked, called for his traveling coach.

His parting shot was for Charlotte. "As for you, young woman, since you made a debacle of this tour, and brought in fewer than the required five paying clients, I will remind you of the terms of our contract. You forfeit the promised sixty-five pounds, which I will keep in my pocket. And," he added, as he followed his portmanteau and the porter out to the inn yard, "should I live to be a hundred, it is my ardent hope that I never again hear the name Pelham."

The gentleman's coachman prompted the horses, who set off at a gallop, heading back to London, and within the half hour Charlotte and Jonathan were saying their farewells to Colonel Fitzgibbon, Russell Thorne, and the Vinton brothers. The four ramblers departed by hired coach, and on the morrow, Charlotte and her one and only brother boarded a westbound stage whose destination was Lancashire.

The journey westward was far from comfortable, with Jonathan nursing a sore shin and Charlotte nursing a broken heart. Though she sympathized with her brother's discomfort, she had every confidence that his shin would soon mend. As for her heart, she doubted that organ would ever be whole again.

Harrison Montgomery had been too concerned about the welfare of his long-lost brother to pay more than scant attention to the ramblers as they each took their leave of him. Earlier, however, he had thanked them profusely for their assistance with Peter. Holding four of the haversacks between, the men had made a sort of makeshift stretcher on which to carry the injured lad the two miles to the apothecary's shop at Wensley. The stretcher had been Charlotte's idea, and it had proven most beneficial in moving the lad without adding to his pain.

As for Charlotte, Harrison had only just begun to speak with her when the apothecary signaled to him to join him in the examining room where Peter lay. Eager to be with his brother, Harrison gave Charlotte the message for Benizur, then said, "Please inform the squire and Mrs. Newsome that I will write to them as soon as I know the extent of Peter's injury. And be so good as to assure them that they need have no fear, for I will remain by my brother's side every moment. When he is fit to travel, I will return with him to Burley. We will talk at that time."

We? Did he mean "we" the squire and his lady, or "we" he and Charlotte?

Unfortunately, he gave her no time to ask; he merely squeezed her hand, then turned and hurried to his brother's bedside.

He had squeezed her hand. Not even the most romantic-minded of females could interpret *that* as the farewell of a lover, nor even of a particular friend. But then, Charlotte had no reason to believe that Harrison felt either love or friendship for her. It mattered little at all that she had given her heart to him and that she would never love another. If Harrison did not love her, then there was no more to be said on the subject.

What could she say? "Excuse me, handsome, thoroughly lovable man, but shall we try our luck at a footrace? The prize? Simple. If you win, I congratulate you. If I win, you marry me."

Naturally she could say nothing of the kind! No man wanted a woman who was so totally lacking in feminine charm, and Harrison, by his own admission, had high standards where a wife was concerned. More's the pity! For Charlotte knew deep in her soul that she could make him happy.

The trip home to Burley took two and a half days, and by the time Charlotte and Jonathan arrived in the village, the disappointed young lady hoped never to see the inside of another stagecoach. She and her brother were greeted with hugs and kisses by their mother, while the vicar and his four young children made them welcome once again in the cramped vicarage.

Not once during the next three weeks did the Vicar or Mrs. Williams take Charlotte to task over the loss of the sixty-five pounds that was to have sent Jonathan to Cambridge. Nor did either of them mention the need for her to seek other employment. In fact, it was their continued cheerfulness—their joy in their wedded bliss and in each other's company—that made Charlotte want to be anyplace but there.

Anyplace! For that reason, when she received a letter from Julia Griswall, asking if she would like to join her ladyship for a month or two at her home in Kent, Charlotte fairly leaped at the chance to get away.

She had replied in the affirmative to the invitation, and was in the process of choosing the clothing to be packed in her trunk, when one of her stepfather's parishioners stopped by on the pretext of returning a book of sermons borrowed from the vicar's library. Not that anyone was fooled by the pretense, for the woman was an inveterate gossip, and her true purpose for visiting the new Mrs. Williams was to deliver the latest news from the village.

"There is a visitor," the maid of all work informed Charlotte. "Mrs. Quinlin."

Though she groaned inwardly, Charlotte thanked the servant for delivering the message. "Be so good as to tell my mother that I will be down directly."

Assuming the subject of the parishioner's visit would once again be Queen Caroline's return to England after her six-year sojourn in Europe—a topic Charlotte felt had been more than exhausted—she did not hurry to the small, slightly worn parlor. When she finally went below stairs, her mother sat in one of the room's leather-covered wing chairs, her expression not unlike that of a polite tree. Though nothing about Mrs. Williams's manner could be called encouraging, the visitor appeared not to notice. She was deep in conversation, so deep she merely waved her greeting to Charlotte, without even pausing for breath.

"It was ever such a fine chaise," Mrs. Quinlin said. "Black with silver trim, and the four horses, though probably job cattle hired on the road, were first quality."

Because Mrs. Quinlin related all gossip as though she had see or heard it personally, Charlotte paid no particular attention to the description of the equipage and horses, which might well have been second- or third-hand information. Instead, she let her mind wander as it wished, and as usual, the person upon whom her thoughts settled was Harrison Montgomery.

"Of course, I don't mind telling you, Mrs. Williams, that I got quite a start when the servant climbed down from the chaise. Though I am persuaded the dear vicar, who we all know is a saint on this earth, would say it behooves us to accept all God's children just as He chose to make them, I do not scruple to tell you, ma'am, that the fellow must surely be the oddest-looking creature the Heavenly Father ever made."

Mrs. Williams, not wanting to encourage conversation her new husband might dislike, merely nodded and asked the visitor if she would care for another macaroon.

"Don't mind if I do, ma'am."

Mrs. Quinlin ate the confection in two bites; then, after pressing the napkin to her lips, she continued as if she had never been interrupted.

Charlotte was lost in her recollection of the assembly at the Eagle Inn, when she had worn Lady Griswall's beautiful cherry red satin evening gown. Once in every woman's life she should be the bell of the ball; that had been Charlotte's night. It had been a wonderful assembly, made even more so by the fact that one of the local gentlemen had erred in the dance and bumped squarely into Charlotte. The delightful result of that encounter was that Harrison had slipped his rock-hard arm around Charlotte's waist and pulled her close against him to keep her from falling.

She could still remember the strength of his arm and the feel of his muscular body against hers. The experience had been heavenly, and in order to stretch it several extra seconds, Charlotte had pretended rather shamelessly that she was unable immediately to regain her balance.

She closed her eyes now to enhance the recollection of being in Harrison's arms, but she was shocked back to the present by the village gossip's next words.

"When I say the man was odd-looking, Mrs. Williams, believe me, I do not exaggerate, for he was small, perhaps no more than five feet tall, and his skin was quite swarthy. His visage was nothing compared to his clothing, however, for he wore a blue silk turban with a jeweled broach pinned just above his forehead, and beneath a long white coat of some kind, his limbs were encased in equally blue silk breeches."

Halfway through the description, Charlotte lost the ability to breathe, for she knew on the instant that the person being described was Benizur. And if the little man was here in Burley, so, too, was Harrison.

Unable to remain silent, she said, "Was the servant the only person you saw, Mrs. Quinlin?"

Charlotte did not dare look at her mother, for she knew what that lady would say about encouraging gossip. Even so, she waited eagerly for the reply. She would take the scold later, but for now she *had* to know if Harrison was in Burley. He had said he would bring Peter home, but there had been no word from him since the first letter to the Newsomes. At least, that was the only letter Charlotte knew about.

Feeling under obligation to visit the squire and Mrs. Newsome at New House on the very day she returned, to tell them about Peter's accident, Charlotte had traveled the half mile that separated the vicarage from their estate. Naturally, the boy's parents had been devastated by the news, and for that reason Charlotte had felt quite justified in dropping by one afternoon a full week later, to see if they had received the promised letter, which they had.

Unfortunately, she could think of no valid reason for visiting New House the following week. Neighborly concern was one thing; poking her nose in someone else's affairs was quite another.

The Newsomes' initial concern for their son's health was alleviated by the letter, in which the apothecary assured them that the lad would be fine as five pence in a matter of days. The secondary fear in their eyes had been put there by the information that their beloved son's wealthy brother had sought and found him. They gave voice to none of their concerns, at least, not within Charlotte's hearing. Even so, she could imagine what must be going through their minds.

At some time or other, adoptive parents must wonder how their son or daughter would react if confronted by a member of his or her birth family. Would the child remain loyal to his second family? Or would he turn his back on the parents who had reared him, to embrace the birth family?

"The servant," Mrs. Quinlin said in answer to Charlotte's question, "was the only one who climbed down from the chaise. He stepped into the apothecary shop for a minute or so, and while he was gone, I got an excellent look at the two who remained inside the coach. You will be surprised, I am sure, Miss Pelham, to hear that one of the occupants was none other than Peter Newsome."

Charlotte held her breath. "And the other?"

"Charlotte!" Mrs. Williams said, no longer able to keep silent. "You will be so good as to ask no more questions."

"That's perfectly all right, ma'am," their visitor assured her. "I was curious myself." Returning her attention to her more receptive listener, she said, "The other gentleman—and gentleman he surely must be, judging by the elegance of his chaise—was a stranger. A very handsome one, I might add, with light brown hair and gray eyes, and—"

Charlotte heard no more. It was not necessary, for she knew the man to be Harrison Montgomery. He had said he would come to bring Peter home to Burley, and he had kept his word. But had he come only to see the Newsomes, or would he remember that Charlotte lived there as well?

Chapter Seventeen

When the handsome black-and-silver chaise came to a stop outside the neat yet unpretentious portico of New House, it did not enter Harrison's head that Charlotte Pelham might be fearful that he would come and go without remembering that she lived in the neighborhood. One glance at Squire Newsome and his lady, however, and Harrison realized they were petrified that he had come only to tell them that he was leaving again and taking their son with him.

The middle-aged couple were short, plump, and rather ordinary-looking, with none of the striking good looks Anne and Thomas James had passed on to their son, Timmy. Even so, Harrison liked the pair on sight.

Their reception of him was cool in the extreme, but he understood perfectly what they must have been feeling. They probably viewed him as a usurper—the instrument by which their hearts would be broken—while Harrison looked upon them with the deepest admiration. His brother was a kind, thoughtful young man, and Harrison knew without a doubt that the lad's character had nothing whatever to do with his birth parents, and everything to do with the terrified couple who stood before him.

Peter hurried beneath the portico to meet them, gathering the tearful lady in his arms and exchanging an emotion-filled handshake with the squire. Moments later, he ushered his parents toward Harrison, who had remained beside the coach to give the family a moment's privacy. "Mother. Father," the lad said, pride in voice. "You will have guessed the identity of this very impressive fellow, but allow me to present to you my older brother, Mr. Harrison Montgomery."

Greetings were exchanged; then the travelers were asked if they would like time to go to their rooms. When they both declined, they were invited into New House's elegant blue-and-cream drawing room.

The tea tray was laden with all of Peter's favorite foods, but understandably enough, he was the only one of the four who managed to swallow more than a few sips of the pungent tea. The Newsomes looked as though even one bite of solid food might send them to early graves, and Harrison was far too concerned with getting the initial meeting over to want anything to eat.

Thankfully, the ordeal did not last long, for Peter was eager to walk over to the vicarage to see how his best friend got on. "Jonathan will want to hear all about my brother and the adventures we had traveling together. Do you mind, Mother?"

"Of course not," Mrs. Newsome said, a forced smile on her face. "I am persuaded that Charlotte will be happy to see you as well, for she stopped by to inquire after your health. Now she will see for herself that you are fully recovered."

At any other time, Harrison would have been pleased to accompany Peter to the vicarage, for he had several important matters he wished to discuss with Miss Charlotte Pelham. At the moment, however, he needed to remain with the Newsomes so he might speak with them while Peter was not there.

Once the lad was gone, however, it was the squire who spoke first.

"We love him," was all the gentleman managed to say before he was obliged to clear his throat. "From the moment we brought him home to New House, just a thin, shy little boy, he has been our primary joy. Our son. To think of being without him is like a knife in my heart. We—"

"You must understand," Mrs. Newsome said. "He is my child as surely as if I had carried him in my body." Tears slid down her face unheeded. "Please, sir, do not take him from . . . from . . ." She got no further, but hid her face in her hands and cried, the force of the sobs wracking her entire body.

Harrison had known this would be difficult, but he had never guessed how hard the words would be to say. "Ma'am, I beg of you, do not cry. You will make yourself ill."

His entreaty served only to increase the lady's sobs, and when he could endure it no longer, Harrison went to her. Getting down on his knees beside her chair, he eased her hands from her face. "Please, ma'am, there is no need for this pain. If you will allow me to speak."

When she tried valiantly to stem the flow of tears, but failed, Harrison took out his handkerchief and dabbed gently at her wet cheeks. "I am fully aware that you have no reason to trust me or my word, ma'am, but I, too, love my brother. I never stopped loving him. For the past twelve years, my one dream has been to return to England to find him."

"Of . . . Of course you love him," the lady said between snuffles. "Anyone who knows him must do so, for he is just that sort of boy."

"But we love him, too," the squire added, his voice suspiciously hoarse.

"Just as he loves you," Harrison said. "In the past

three weeks, my brother has told me so much about his life here in Burley, and about the closeness of your family. To hear him speak is to know that he holds you both in the highest esteem. No boy could have asked for better parents, and I will not insult you by thanking you for giving Peter such a wonderful childhood."

"*Humph*," was the squire's only response.

"What I *do* want," Harrison continued, "is to give you my assurance that I have no wish to cause you the least distress. I do not mean to take Peter from you. I could not if I wanted to. Believe me, he made that perfectly clear."

"He . . . He did?"

"Yes, ma'am. A very stubborn young man is Peter Newsome."

Since this unflattering remark had the effect of making the lady laugh, Harrison was encouraged to continue. "Why, every other sentence was 'My mother this,' and 'My father that,' until I was quite ready to strangle the lad."

The squire was obliged to find his own handkerchief, and after a rather noisy blow, he said, "He is a good boy."

"The best," Harrison agreed, "and for that I will thank you."

Harrison hesitated, for though he had not the least doubt that the Newsomes loved his brother, he had no way of knowing how they would accept his proposal. "Sir, ma'am, I have but one request, and that is that you allow me to visit Peter from time to time. If not here in Burley, then at some place of your choosing. You cannot know what it would mean to me."

"You wish only to visit with him?" Mrs. Newsome said. "You truly do not mean to take him away?"

"As if I could. The lad tells me he would be lost

without your love and guidance, and his happiness is of prime importance to me. How could I wish to deprive him of the only family he has ever known?''

After another, even louder blow, the squire got up from his chair, crossed the handsome blue-and-gold Axminster carpet, then gave the tapestry bellpull a hearty yank. The butler appeared on the instant, took the order for a bottle of the squire's best champagne and three glasses, then bowed himself out of the room.

Once they were alone again, the squire said, ''Tea is all well and good in its place, but I feel the need for something a bit stronger, and I venture to say you do, too, my boy.''

''Yes, sir,'' Harrison replied, happy to know the worst of the meeting was over.

Once the champagne arrived, and the three of them drank a toast to Peter, and another to reunited brothers, the squire asked his wife which bedchamber she had had prepared for Mr. Montgomery's visit.

''The green,'' she replied.

''Ah, yes, of course,'' her spouse said. He appeared to be mulling something over in his mind. When he came to a decision, he said, ''The green will do for the night I suppose, but we cannot have our boy's brother sleeping in the guest wing.''

A look passed between the couple; then the lady nodded her head. ''Definitely not the guest wing. I think the suite next to Peter's will do nicely. Brothers ought to be close enough so they can pop in and out of one another's rooms. They cannot be forever running from wing to wing when they have something they wish to discuss.''

Harrison could not believe it; he was being given one of the family suites, almost as if . . . ''You are very kind, ma'am.''

"Now, no more of that, my boy. You are Peter's brother, and though my head is too addled at the moment to allow me to think clearly, I am convinced that if you are his family, you must also be ours. I cannot speak for my husband, of course, but I always wanted at least one more son."

"By Jove," the squire said. "An excellent notion, my love. Should have thought of it myself. The lad may be a bit too old for anything legal, you understand, but it wouldn't hurt to see what my solicitor has to say on the subject." He sighed loudly. "Two sons. Devilish good notion that!"

Harrison almost laughed aloud at the idea of an adoption at his age, but when he looked at the sincere faces of his brother's parents, he kept his laugher in check. Theirs was a magnanimous gesture, and he would not cheapen it with so much as a smile.

As if struck by a new idea, the squire said, "I say, my boy, do your friends call you Harry?"

"No, sir, my friends call me Harrison, but I would be pleased if you would call me Sonny."

Chapter Eighteen

Mrs. Quinlin had left the vicarage at least an hour ago, and Charlotte, after having endured a scold from her mother on encouraging gossip, sat on a wrought-iron bench in the wildflower garden to the right of the rectory, absently stripping blue clematis off the vines that practically covered the low garden wall. She knew she should be concentrating on finding some sort of employment that would support her, but all she could think about was Harrison Montgomery and the fact that he was in Burley. Possibly at New House this very minute. Only half a mile away.

Half a mile. She could walk that in a matter of minutes. She could run it in even less! If she acted surprised when they met, Harrison need never know that she had come for no other reason than to see him.

She had all but decided to try her luck when she looked up to see Peter Newsome walking down the lane. Drat! Now she could no longer claim she did not know Harrison was there. Come to think of it, where was he? Certainly not with the younger brother he had escorted home.

"Charlie!" Peter called. "I have returned."

"So I see. And not a minute too soon, for Jonathan is being driven insane by the four little ones, who have decided that his injured shin makes him a hero."

"What? Is the shin no better?"

"Completely, but he still figures as their hero, which means he can go no place without at least half the little ones following him. Since your injury was more serious than his, perhaps the children will transfer the laurel wreath to your head."

"Good-bye," he said, pretending to leave.

The both laughed; then Charlotte asked to be told everything that had happened after she and the four ramblers left Peter at the apothecary's. Naturally, Peter did not supply all the details, but he told her a bit about his recuperation and answered all her questions regarding his reunion with his brother.

"And is Mr. Montgomery with you?" she asked, feeling like the veryest sneak for resorting to subterfuge. At Peter's nod, she asked if the gentleman meant to remain in the neighborhood long enough to renew old acquaintances.

"For heaven's sake, Charlie, if you want to know if he means to visit you, why do you not just come right out and ask."

"I was trying to be subtle."

"Subtle? Why would you want to be subtle?"

Why, indeed? "Because it is the ladylike way to behave. And because I do not want to give him a disgust of me."

Peter's reaction to that remark was a bark of laughter. "I hardly think that likely. Especially since my brother spent the better part of our drive from Yorkshire to Lancashire asking me all manner of questions about you."

Charlotte's breath caught. "Questions? About me?"

"By the hundreds. The most surprising of which was how long you had been engaged. He seems to think you are in love with someone, and from all I can gather, his major reason for escorting me to Burley is so he can murder your alleged fiancé on sight."

Murder! Charlotte sighed. What a lovely word.

She had not the first clue that Harrison felt anything but friendship for her, and at the thought of him caring enough to be jealous, a smile pulled at the corners of her mouth. Obviously she had been mistaken about him finding it difficult to believe that anyone else would find her attractive. When he had asked her if she was engaged and she had refused to reply, he must have taken her silence for an affirmative answer. And now, here he was in Burley, ready to do murder.

Charlotte felt an almost uncontrollable urge to do cartwheels. Instead, she sat on the low wall, swung her legs over to the other side, and hopped down. "When you go inside," she said, "tell my mother that I have gone to New House."

"Charlie, for heaven's sake. I thought you were trying to be subtle."

"I did try it, but I find I do not like it."

"But you are not even wearing a hat."

"As if I care."

"You may not, but I wager your mother will."

"That cannot be helped, for if I sit around here acting ladylike for one more minute, there is every chance I will end my days a Bedlamite. So, to save my sanity, I am going to act like me. And I mean to start by finding the man I love."

Peter shook his head. "And when you find him?"

Charlotte smiled, remembering what she had once told herself she could never say. "When I find him, I will say, 'Handsome man, I hereby challenge you to a footrace.'"

Fortunately for Charlotte's sanity, she met Harrison in the lane, halfway between the vicarage and New House. He was on his way to find her. Just watching him walk toward her, his long strides seeming to eat up the distance that separated them, made her pulses quicken. He wore a slate-gray coat that fit his broad shoulders to perfection, and pale blue breeches that gave evidence of the strength of his legs, and he had never looked more handsome.

She had almost forgotten how tall he was, and just looking at his smiling face made her heart beat so loud she wondered if Mrs. Quinlin could hear it back in the village. Would she and Harrison figure as tomorrow's gossip? Charlotte sincerely hoped so.

Reaching her at last, he said, "What are you doing here?"

"Oh," she said nonchalantly, "just out for a bit of exercise."

"Liar," he said, laughing aloud. "Admit it. You came to meet me."

"And if I did?"

"If you did," he said quietly, "then I think you deserve a reward."

The softly spoken words sent waves of awareness all along Charlotte's skin. Delightful awareness. "What sort of reward?"

"You name it," he said. Slowly he reached his hand out and touched her cheek. When she did not move away, he slipped his fingers into her hair, so that he cupped the back of her head. "Would a kiss do?"

"Oh, yes. A kiss would do very nicely."

As he had done once before, he put his finger beneath her chin and lifted her face; then he bent his head and brushed his lips ever so gently against hers.

The magic was there again, only stronger than ever, and Charlotte positively ached to wrap her arms around his neck and kiss him back. Feeling uncharacteristically shy, she said, "That was lovely. May I, er . . ."

"May you what?"

"May I kiss you?"

A slow smile worked its way from his mouth to those mysterious gray eyes, and Charlotte wondered how a simple upward turn of his lips could make her knees feel as boneless as India rubber. "Madam," he said, "you may do with me what you will."

She felt warm all over, but she did not let that stop her from placing her hands on his chest. When she felt the beat of his heart beneath her right palm, the sensation so mesmerized her that to remove her hand would have left her feeling desolate. With one hand on his chest, she slowly eased the other hand up and over his shoulders. Finally, she wrapped her left arm around his neck and urged his head down to meet hers.

At first, she pressed her lips against his, softly, as he had done to her. He did not move, but let her kiss him in whatever way pleased her. Encouraged by his good-natured acquiescence, she kissed him a second time, though not quite so softly as before.

With her arm around his neck, he was so close Charlotte could feel the heat of his body, and for a time that pleased her very well. With the third kiss, however, she pressed her chest against his, and at the sound of his indrawn breath, she knew exactly what she wanted.

"Put your arms around me," she said, "and we will both kiss at once."

Never a man to pass up such an offer, Harrison caught her around the waist and pulled her close against him, molding the full length of her soft, healthy body to his. This time when he claimed her lips, he kissed her deeply, as he had wanted to for as long as he could remember. And to his delight, his beloved answered him kiss for kiss.

Charlotte Pelham kissed as she did everything else,

with her entire heart and soul, and before Harrison quite knew how it had happened, her innocent exuberance had enflamed him almost beyond endurance. Knowing he had better stop while he still could, he eased away from her, softening the blow of separation with tiny kisses on her nose and her eyelids.

"Do we have to stop?" she asked, her voice delightfully breathless.

"Yes, my love," he replied, his own voice none too steady. "I fear we must."

"But I was enjoying it."

Harrison looked down into her kiss-flushed face and very nearly lost his resolve. It was fortunate they stood in the middle of a public lane, where anyone might walk by; otherwise, he might have given in to the temptation of those soft, pink lips.

"My beautiful nymph," he whispered, gently removing her arm from around his neck, "I told you I was no gentleman, and before you make me forget even those few scruples I possess, there is a question I must ask you."

To his delight, she chuckled. "Actually, there is one I have been longing to ask you."

"Oh, and what might that be?"

"Will you accept a challenge?"

"Yes. If you like."

She smiled then, and there was such a look of devilment in her dark eyes that Harrison was hard pressed not to take her in his arms and kiss her again. "I challenge you to a footrace," she said. "If you win, you may name your prize."

"And if *you* win this footrace? What then?"

"If I win, sir, you must marry me."

"Hmm," he said, as if needing to consider the proposition. "It is an interesting challenge, to be sure, but I am not at all happy with the inequality of the prizes."

Her eyes widened. "No? Tell me, sir, how do you propose to make them more equal?"

Propose. Now there was an interesting choice of words. "Since you would have it that if *you* win, I must marry you, the only fair thing would be that if *I* win, you must marry *me* and allow me to take you to Egypt for that camel ride."

"To Egypt? Truly? Oh, Harrison, how marvelous. When may we go?"

"The day after our wedding."

"Excellent!" Charlotte said. "And since you are being such a gentleman about everything, I forfeit the footrace, and herewith declare you to be the winner this very instant. You may claim your prize as soon as you like."

"One month from today?"

"One month from today," she said, "and I will even supply the vicar."

"Darling girl, has anyone ever told you what a gracious loser you are?"

"Never." She laughed then, a happy sound that fairly stole Harrison's heart away. "No one has ever said it, because I never lose. Except this once, of course. And now, because I *am* such a gracious loser, do you not think I deserve another of those special rewards?"

Without so much as a by-your-leave, Charlotte slipped her arms around his waist and turned her face up for his kiss. "Reward me, if you please, my darling husband-to-be."

Realizing it was his turn to be a gracious winner, Harrison gathered her close and kissed her. Then he kissed her again. And again. And again.

Author's Note

There is actually a cross-country walking trail that begins at St. Bee's Head, on the Irish Sea, and ends at Robin Hood's Bay, on the North Sea. The one-hundred-ninety-mile walk is as popular today as it was in the nineteenth century, and though the more intrepid nature lovers often travel the route on their own, fourteen-day guided tours are available.

Though the route of the cross-country ramble in this book was loosely based on present-day walks, many of the outdoor incidents used were told to me by a seasoned hiker and climber, who is also an instructor with both the New York Outward Bound and the Pacific Coast Outward Bound. The motto of that wonderful organization is, "To serve, to strive, and not to yield," and I chose that for my heroine's personal credo.

Thank you, Lenny, Lara, and Dawn Ellen.

Signet Regency Romances

THE MAGNIFICENT MARQUESS
by Gail Eastwood

Recently returned from India, the new Marquess of Milbourne was the darling of the *ton*, with half the eligible ladies of the city in vigorous pursuit of his undying devotion. But the handsome young man harbored a dark secret that had made him vow never to love again...

❑ 0-451-19532-9/$4.99

THE BEST INTENTIONS
by Candice Hern

When Miles Prescott's formidable sister Winifred descends upon Epping Manor with two eligible women in tow, the widowed earl knows his single days are numbered; but when he ends up being attracted to the sister of the woman everyone expects him to marry, things become a bit more complicated...

❑ 0-451-19573-6/$4.99

LORD DRAGONER'S WIFE
by Lynn Kerstan

When the scandalous Lord Dragoner returns to England, Delilah's hopes of a reconciliation are shattered. The husband who coldly abandoned her has come to seek a divorce. But she is determined to win his heart, even if it means joining him in the dangerous world where no one can be trusted—not even his wife.

❑ 0-451-19861-1/$4.99

To order call: 1-800-788-6262

Explore the World of Signet Regency Romance

Emma Jensen

"One of my favorites, the best of a new generation of Regency writers." —Barbara Metzger

❑ THE IRISH ROGUE   0-451-19873-5/$4.99

Laura Matthews

❑ A PRUDENT MATCH   0-451-20070-5/$4.99

Barbara Metzger

"One of the genre's wittiest pens." —*Romantic Times*

❑ THE PAINTED LADY   0-451-20368-2/$4.99
❑ MISS WESTLAKE'S WINDFALL   0-451-20279-1/$4.99
❑ SAVED BY SCANDAL   0-451-20038-1/$4.99

To order call: 1-800-788-6262